THE ENGLISH NOVEL

BENN'S ESSEX LIBRARY

Edited by Edward G. Hawke, M.A.

J. B. PRIESTLEY

THE ENGLISH NOVEL

LONDON: ERNEST BENN LTD.

Bouverie Ho. e, Fleet Street.

Republished 1971
Scholarly Press, Inc., 22929 Industrial Drive East
St. Clair Shores, Michigan 48080

First published 1927
Second Impression February 1928
Third Impression March 1928
Fourth Impression (Essex Library) 1931

Library of Congress Catalog Card Number: 75-158906
ISBN 0-403-01311-9

CONTENTS

THE ENGLISH NOVEL

CHAPTER I

INTRODUCTORY

WHAT is a novel? Sometimes people use the term to describe only certain kinds of fiction. Thus, if a story is filled with tea-parties, they will call it " a novel "; but if it is filled with sea fights, they will call it " a romance." When I talk of novels in these chapters, however, I mean any and every kind of fiction. The only definition of the novel I can offer is that it is a narrative in prose treating chiefly of imaginary characters and events. Some novels, such as Scott's *Kenilworth* or Thackeray's *Esmond*, do show us actual historical personages, but nevertheless they all contain far more fiction than fact. It would be extremely difficult

7

to draw a line between the most imaginative pieces of historical writing and the most carefully documented works of historical fiction, but fortunately it is no great matter if such a line is left undrawn. In practice we find it is easy to distinguish between the historians and the novelists. The definition I have given tells us very little about prose fiction, but, then, prose fiction itself, as a whole, tells us so much. It is a large mirror of life, and has a far greater range than any other form of literature. Fiction can be approached and enjoyed in so many different ways that it is almost as bewildering as life itself. I will enumerate some of these ways. We may regard fiction as a narrative pure and simple, or as a picture of manners, or as an exhibition of character, or as the vehicle of a certain philosophy of life. Again, we may approach a novel with none of these things in our minds, but with an intense desire to be more fully acquainted with the personality of the novelist himself, whose every little turn of phrase has a fascination for us. And though we may declare that not all these interests are on the same level, we have no right to say that they do not exist and have nothing to do with fiction. There are critics who tell us that we go to a novel for this or that, whereas in truth they are only telling us what their own interests happen to be. If we examine the criticism of fiction, we discover that it is always insisting upon one particular aspect at the expense of all the others. Here in England, however, throughout many changes of fashion in literature, one standard of judgment in fiction has remained. We English have always had a zest for character, for sharply defined and vivid personalities. It is not surprising, then, that the novel here has always been regarded as a stage for the display of character, and the novelist himself examined by criticism in his capacity as a creator of character. Our great writers of fiction are all very different, but nevertheless they are all alike in this—that they are able to present to us vital figures, in whose exist-

I *

ence, no matter how wild and strange they may be, we are compelled to believe while we are reading.   No novelist who has had the power of creating interesting characters has failed to win a place of importance for himself or herself.   If one single test is to be applied to fiction, then this of character is undoubtedly the safest, for we may be sure that it will never admit a bad novelist nor exclude a really good one.   But there is no reason why we should look for one single test.   The art of fiction, like life itself, is too complicated for that; and as, in practice, we apply all manner of tests to the novel, it would be absurd to limit ourselves in theory to one of them, even though it should be the surest.

In the account of the English Novel that follows, an account that is necessarily limited, I have made use of the chronological method because that is easily the most convenient. On the other hand, I have not tried to present a history pure and simple of English fiction. Indeed, I have tried to avoid the usual weak-

nesses of historical treatment. Critics who
work with their eyes fixed on the development of the Novel are apt to mislead their
readers in one of two different ways. The
first set of critics fall into the error of treating
an art as if it were a science. A scientist can
accept the conclusions of some previous
worker in the same field, and then proceed
with his own research, and thus one generation of scientists can, as it were, cancel out
former generations. But this is not true of
artists, who must always begin all over again.
The science of chemistry is not what it was
in the eighteenth century, and the art of
fiction is not what it was when Fielding
wrote, but that does not mean that the
eighteenth-century chemist and Fielding are
on the same level. The chemist's text-book
is long out of date, but Fielding's novels are
not out of date. A Henry James carries the
art of fiction into regions that a Scott never
knew, but that does not mean that we have
now done with Scott. But some critics,
overlooking the fact that art cannot swallow

all that went before as science can, make each generation of writers cancel out the one before until at last it appears that the only novelists worth reading are those whose works are still hot from the press. The art of fiction itself develops because it does actually come to conquer more and more territory, but the individual novel or novelist does not develop in this way. Something is gained, something lost. If the novelists of to-day are busy exploring the dim recesses of their characters' minds, then you may be sure they are not giving us the movement and sweep, the broad comprehensive action, of the novelists of yesterday.

The second set of critics, more common in this country, perhaps, and certainly more conspicuous as historians of fiction, fall into the opposing error. They would seem to believe that it is by its roots and not by its fruits that we shall know an art. They produce histories of the novel that squander whole chapters in pursuit of dim origins, and then have little or no space left for the novel proper when it arrives. Such pieces of research may be exceedingly valuable to the student, but they should be renamed : they are histories of the origins of the English Novel. Not unconnected with this is that other weakness of the literary historian, a tendency to allow historical interests to dominate purely critical interests. The critic, instead of saying what he himself really feels about a writer, will put himself at the point of view of a past generation of readers, and will quite honestly praise a book that he could never have read through if he had not had to write about it. In the account that follows I have tried to avoid this common fault of the literary historian, and to survey our fiction from the point of view of an ordinary intelligent reader of our own time : the novelists are estimated according to their value to us, here and now. I shall not give biographical details, except where the criticism demands their assistance, because space is valuable, and there are plenty of reference books that supply such details.

Having now divested ourselves of one or other of those two snobberies of chronology, the belief that the old must be better than the new, or the new must be better than the old, we are ready to begin. The door stands open; we can enter the treasure-house.

CHAPTER II

THE Middle Ages can show us prose narratives, chief of them the famous *Morte d'Arthur*, the legends retold by Sir Thomas Malory. The sixteenth century had its fictions, from which Shakespeare took some of his plots. There was John Lyly's *Euphues*, in two parts, both of which have some pretensions to story-telling, but are in reality little more than dialogues written in a most elaborate and tortured style. There was Sidney's *Arcadia*, a pastoral romance containing a good deal of incident but very little character, all remote and dream-like; it is really a poem smoothed out into prose. There was Lodge's *Rosalynde*, a pretty faded tale that Shakespeare quickens into life in *As You Like It*. And, not least, there was Nashe's *The Unfortunate Traveller, or the Life*

15

of Jacke Wilton, which has no unity as a tale, but has the merit of escaping from dreamland and coming close to real life. The seventeenth century is the age of heroic romances, for the most part imitations of Continental models, those very long-winded and extravagant narratives that Cervantes laughed at (while laughing at a great many other, and more important, things) in *Don Quixote*, which is, perhaps, the best story in the world. There is no space here in which to discuss these romances, *Parthenissa*, *Aretina*, *Pandion and Amphigenia*, and the rest; it is sufficient to say that they do not represent the beginning of something new, but the last long-drawn gasps of something old and dying. Women tried their hand at them, and one woman, Mrs. Aphra Behn, in her *Oroonoko* and *The Fair Jilt*, did succeed in taking leave of that vague realm of fine names and interminable speeches and in making some approach to reality. But a more entertaining story-teller than any of his contemporaries was the one man who would have shuddered at hearing himself so described, and that was John Bunyan.   Bunyan was not trying to write fiction, but to preach a sermon; he did not aim at creating characters, but merely at personifying vices and virtues; yet the fact remains that the creatures of his allegories, Mr. Worldly Wiseman and Mr. Badman, Faithful and Christian, are more like human beings than the figures in all the prose romances of his time.   The background of his narratives may be abstract, but the foreground is full of homely concrete things.

It was the age that followed, however, that produced the novel proper.   The first name of any real importance in any chronicle of English fiction is that of Daniel Defoe (1661–1731), a man of a not unfamiliar type, who tried his hand at all manner of things, and finally became what we should now call a journalist.   The stories of the previous ages cannot escape the charge of being obviously unreal; we do not believe in them for a moment.   The merit of Defoe is that he achieved the complete illusion of reality, so complete, indeed, that for many years some of his inventions, supposed auto-biographies such as his *Memories of a Cavalier*, were thought to be the memoirs of real people. There is hardly any device for creating the illusion of reality that he did not employ, and employ successfully. He gets inside the skin of his fictitious narrators, Robinson Crusoe, Colonel Jack, Moll Flanders, and the rest, keeps himself entirely out of sight, goes solemnly from one little fact to the next with an apparent artlessness that is really artfulness itself, so that we are compelled to believe. Our imagination is captured, not by some splendid thrusts of poetry or humour, but by the constant nibbling of his little facts. In *Robinson Crusoe*, his masterpiece, Defoe had an ideal subject. It is a romance that might have come out of a box of tools. Crusoe is naked humanity seen grappling with its most homely and yet most urgent problems. Defoe's very limitations—for it is certain that he could not have added any poetic colouring of romance even if he had wished to do so—were a help and not a hindrance in this tale of the man on the island.   No tale had ever less picturesque decoration, depended more upon simple facts, and yet it remains one of the great romantic stories of the world. Crusoe himself is completely in character; even his moralising, which gives us some very dull passages, particularly when he has done with the island, seems part of the man. Defoe's minor novels are not so good—though they are still worth reading—because they have not the unity given to Crusoe by its simple but magnificent theme, and are apt to degenerate into drab rambling chronicles; but they, too, have this supreme reality and this dependence upon homely fact, a quality in the narration that has made his fiction equally appealing to children and unsophisticated persons and to some of our greatest romantic writers.

This quality may be found in the work of a giant contemporary of Defoe's who can hardly be considered a novelist. It is significant that Swift's *Gulliver's Travels*, one of the most savage satires on the human race that has ever appeared, has long been a favourite book with children. It is, of course, only the first two voyages, to Lilliput and Brobdingnag, that interest children, who are fascinated by the grave accounts of Gulliver as a giant among pigmies, or as a pigmy among giants. Here, again, it is the solemn verisimilitude, the accumulation of significant facts, that take hold of the imagination. Whether we are among the pigmies or the giants, the strictest proportion is maintained, and one delightful detail after another is brought out by the narrator, who keeps the gravest of faces throughout the recital. We cannot call Swift a novelist, but any account of the novel would pay tribute to his astonishing powers of realistic narrative. Nor, of course, can we call the two essayists, Steele and Addison, novelists, but they deserve a word because the excellent humorous character-drawing in their sketches of Sir Roger de Coverley, Will Honeycomb, Captain Sentry, Will Wimble, and the others, are close to fiction, and to fiction of a very fine quality. Here we have character, real character at last, closely observed and humorously and affectionately portrayed: Sir Roger and his friends are not simply satirical pieces of description, mere bundles of traits, but are humorously alive, smiling at us from the page. The little essays that tell us about these people are like selections, episodes, chosen at random, from some great unwritten novel. Combine with this character-drawing and delicious treatment of episodes Defoe's power of sustained and realistic story-telling, and you have the novel in full strength. Nor have we long to wait.

The name that must follow Defoe's is that of a little fat bookseller who did not turn novelist until he was past fifty. This was Samuel Richardson (1689–1761), whose works were soon famous, not only in England, but all over the Continent. There was a new reading public, chiefly composed of women of the middle classes, rapidly springing up, and Richardson captured it. He also captured some of the most famous men of his time : Diderot, for example, put him beside Homer and Euripides. In all his three novels, *Pamela*, *Clarissa Harlowe*, and *Sir Charles Grandison*, the method, the manner, the very atmosphere, are the same. They are told in letters, frequently of such preposterous length that the writers would have had to be scribbling day and night in order to produce them at all. Never were twenty-fours longer than they are in Richardson's novels. They are almost entirely concerned with the conflict between feminine chastity or prudence and masculine licentiousness (though Sir Charles Grandison is, perhaps, the greatest prig known to literature); and the actual stories they have to tell are really very slight, particularly when compared with the time it takes to tell them. " If you were to read Richardson for the story," Dr. Johnson remarked, " your impatience would be so much fretted that you would hang yourself. But you must read him for the sentiment, and consider the story as giving occasion to the sentiment." This gives us the key. What Richardson did, in fact, was to produce a slow-motion picture of human life on its purely sentimental side. His heroines, especially Clarissa, suffer through volume after volume, in which not a sob nor a tear is overlooked in the record. The long letters from each character in turn compel us to share their every hope and fear. We have to spend a week of our own time to spend, perhaps, a day of theirs. It is not difficult to understand Richardson's vast popularity. His readers, who had never been asked by any novelist before to share so liberally in the feelings of his people, told one another that Richardson was a great creator, who had the power of putting the human heart under a microscope. His sentiment was their sentiment, and here was God's plenty. Moreover, Richardson, who spent far more of his time among women than among men, and who regularly received their confidences, was only too willing to give his feminine audience what they wanted : he was capable of devoting a whole volume to a description of the preparations for a wedding. There is, indeed, something curiously feminine about him. Sir Charles Grandison is a sanctimonious spinster's idea of a fine gentleman, though Lovelace, the villain of the piece in *Clarissa Harlowe*, is something more than the same lady's idea of a wicked fellow. His strength as a story-teller lies in his massive deliberation, his huge but perfectly steady movement, his power of adding stroke to stroke; once he really catches the interest, he has it in a vice-like grip. But with each passing generation it has become more and more difficult for him to catch that interest; no novelist who has been given so much praise is now so seldom read. There are many reasons for this, and among them the fact that he demands more leisure than most people are willing or able to give, and the further fact that the absurdities of his method have only been thrown into relief by the succeeding development of the Novel. But what has chiefly betrayed him to time is the quality of his mind, which is not that of a great novelist. Much of that sentiment with which he made such play now rings false. Much of his material is not that enduring stuff of human nature which enables the writer who can make use of it to walk serenely from age to age. What seemed fine morality to him and his readers now appears mere cant. His first heroine, Pamela, a servant girl who is persecuted by her young master because he wants to seduce her, but who eludes him so successfully that at last he marries her, seems to us a rather sly chit. She was only transformed into an admirable heroine by the curious unhealthy hot-house atmosphere that envelopes all Richardson's novels.

It was Henry Fielding (1707–1754) who smashed a few panes of glass and let the cool air into that hot-house. He had written a few indifferent comedies and some miscellaneous things when the success of *Pamela* tempted him to parody it in a story of his own. Richardson had given his readers the history of a virtuous servant girl who resisted her master's attempts to seduce her; so Fielding produced a virtuous footman who equally resisted the attempts of his mistress to seduce him. This was the origin of his first novel, *Joseph Andrews;* but once Fielding had set his characters in motion he did not trouble himself about the parody, but aimed at producing what he called a comic epic poem in prose. This he did again, at greater length and far more elaborately, in his *Tom Jones*, one of the most massive works in all English fiction. He lived long enough to produce a third novel, *Amelia;* and in addition he wrote a *History of the Life of the late Mr. Jonathan Wild the Great*, in which the exploits of that rascal are celebrated in the epic style. There is no more grimly ironical narrative in our whole literature than this *Jonathan Wild;* and only those with a decided relish for irony are likely to enjoy this sustained mock apprecia-

tion of villainy.   In this tale Fielding is the
moralist pure and simple; what he is saying
throughout is what really marks the vital
difference between men is the absence or
presence of the good will, or goodness of
heart; set this apart, and there is no reason
why you should not have an enthusiastic
biography of Mr. Wild. Fielding carried
this simple morality, which, in opposition
to much of the current morality of his time,
stresses the will to do good instead of the
mere observance of a code, into his novels
proper; but he carried into them a great deal
more.   The irony is there too, ever present,
and sometimes so subtle, so profound, that
stupid readers are unaware of its existence,
and imagine that a man who has too much
brain for their comprehension has not
enough to amuse them.   But in addition
there is humour, a magnificent comic narrative power, and a robust sense of character.
The first novel, *Joseph Andrews*, is comparatively slight, but it glows with health
and vitality.   It takes us wandering with

Joseph and his girl and their unsophisticated friend, Parson Adams, easily the greatest character in the book, up and down the roads of England; and throughout the comic misadventures, the horse-play and buffetings, there shines a steady light that brings into relief at every other moment some different phase of our common nature. Nothing could be better of its kind than the delightful irony that plays like summer lightning round the figure of the absent-minded, foolish, gentle, heroic Parson Adams.

Tom Jones shows us the same world, but presents it on an epic scale. " What a master of composition Fielding was ! " cried Coleridge, who declared that *Tom Jones* was one " of the three most perfect plots ever planned." And Gibbon, calling it " that exquisite picture of human manners," said that it would outlive the palace of the Escurial and the imperial eagle of Austria, a prophecy that has been fulfilled in part. Yet the book has been condemned as a vicious production at fairly regular intervals

ever since it was first published.   The fact
is that it is as vicious as a morning's walk
through the nearest town.   Such a walk
might be bad for an invalid, and an acquaintance with *Tom Jones* might be bad for a moral
invalid, but for nobody else.   " It is easier
to make good men wise than to make bad
men good," Fielding declared in his dedica-
tion of the story.   Tom himself is good—in
the sense that, whatever his faults may be, his
impulses are generous and his heart open and
kindly—but he is anything but wise, and
throughout the vast chronicle, in which he
and his Sophia lose and find and lose one
another, we watch him paying for his follies.
There is no escape for him until the very last
chapter.   But this is to talk of the novel as
if it were some cut-and-dried piece of moral
prosing.   Actually it is so stirring with life
that many readers do not notice how closely
knit and logical its action is and probably do
not care, being content to lean back and
enjoy this great panorama of the eighteenth-
century world, its roads and inn parlours and

masquerades and country houses and shabby
town lodgings, and the company of Tom and
his pretty Sophia and Partridge and pert
Mrs. Honour and roaring Squire Western
and all the ostlers and landlords and bullies
and wenches.   But the coarse and hearty
realism that is so obvious in Fielding must
not blind us—as it has done so many readers,
critics among them—to the solid weight of
intellect there is in his fiction, to the never-
ceasing play of his irony.   He has qualities
that lie beyond his robust common sense, his
vast experience of life (he was a London
magistrate and an unusually good one), his
power of presenting comic incident and droll
characters.   As a novelist pure and simple,
he takes rank with our greatest masters.
He has his weaknesses, of course.   Thus, he
made too much of the " comic epic " business, and we weary of his mock-heroic
descriptions of scuffles and horse-play; the
inset story in *Tom Jones* we could well spare,
as, indeed, we could the various intro-
ductions, good as they are; his heroines,

though easily the best of his time, never quite become human beings; and there is a whole range of feeling apparently outside his grasp. But these limitations seem trifling when we consider his genius, which took hold of prose fiction and transformed it into enduring art, giving the Novel the bustle of life itself, and yet also giving it shapeliness and balance and a massive solidity. His characters are alive, and every scene comes before us naturally, and yet he never deviates from his strict purpose. The modern reader has novels enough and to spare at his command, and he may conclude that Fielding, so far away, is not for him. Possibly he may have dipped into *Joseph Andrews* or *Tom Jones* and have been repelled by a certain formality, a feeling that his author is addressing him from under a periwig. Let him try again, reading closely and waiting for the irony, the profound play of humour beneath the surface play of fun, and he will soon discover that he has made friends with a great man.

There was a time when criticism treated
Fielding and Tobias Smollett (1721–1771)
as equals.   In reality there is a gulf between
them : Fielding has genius, and Smollett has
lively talent.   Smollett was content to work
on the surface of life : he had a sharp eye for
oddities of appearance and manner; he knew
the ups and downs of this world; he had a
zest for the bustle of life, for adventure and
buffoonery, and coarse, high spirits; but his
humour is little more than a sense of burl-
esque, his character-drawing is superficial,
his constructive powers are feeble, and there
is something coarse, gritty, about his mind,
which is fundamentally prosaic.   His best
novels are *Roderick Random*, *Peregrine Pickle*,
and *Humphrey Clinker*, and they all belong to
the *picaresque* school (of which the greatest
example is *Gil Blas*) : there is no plot to
speak of, no plan of action; the chief
characters are sent wandering about the
country and meet all manner of odd people
and have all kinds of adventures.   The best
of the three is the last, *Humphrey Clinker*,

which is related in letters by the various characters in turn; there is real humour, as distinct from buffoonery, in some of these letters, and the author's manner is more gentle in this book than it is in the earlier stories. Both Scott and Thackeray, no bad judges, considered *Humphrey Clinker* the most laughable story we have; but it cannot be compared with *Pickwick Papers*, to name no other. It is only fair to Smollett, however, to say that Dickens himself was inspired by his early acquaintance with these bustling chronicles, filled with wayside adventures and grotesque figures and a healthy boyish sense of fun. Indeed, for sixty or seventy years after Smollett's death, novels in his manner poured out from the press.

Once we arrive at the latter half of the eighteenth century, we find the Novel in such favour that every original work is imitated over and over again. Even to begin to discuss these productions would be to fill page after page with useless names and

2

dates. It is enough to remark that the flood of fiction in which we are now almost engulfed had then begun, that there was a large and ever-growing public for novels, and that more and more writers, whether they were industrious hacks or men of literary genius, turned their attention to the form. Among the men of genius—indeed, the greatest of them after Fielding—was Laurence Sterne (1713–1768), a country parson who after many years of idling suddenly astonished the world with *Tristram Shandy*, and then followed it with *A Sentimental Journey*. Sterne is a humorist pure and simple, though—to paraphrase Wilde's epigram—he is rarely pure and never simple. Some time ago a certain film was described by its producers as " the picture that makes the dimples to catch the tears." Sterne, who was a fastidious literary artist, would have shuddered at the phrase; but he would have approved the intention, which was his own. All he wanted was to play, with the most delicate art, upon the feelings of his readers; unlike most of his contemporaries, he had no desire to improve, but only to move his readers, to make them laugh or cry with every added stroke of his pen.   Perhaps no writer has ever juggled more dexterously with humour and pathos.   The title of his second book exactly describes his attitude towards life.   In some ways he was quite unscrupulous;   much of his material is borrowed; his novel, *Tristram Shandy*, is an absurdity because the apparent hero is not born until halfway through; and in addition he plays the most grotesque tricks upon the reader, who must put up with a story that is really all digressions.   But he is, in truth, anything but a mountebank when he is considered as a literary artist.   When we have dismissed the tomfoolery, the silly suggestiveness, the occasional posturing, that make some chapters of *Tristram Shandy* so tedious or irritating, there remain some scenes of humour and delicately finished character-drawing that have never been surpassed. He introduces us into a company of whimsical personages—Walter Shandy, the unfortunate philosopher whose wife and brother can never understand his reasoning, the guileless Uncle Toby and his Corporal Trim, Mrs. Shandy, and Parson Yorick, whom, once we have met, we remember with delight for ever. These people cannot understand one another—in which fact lies so much of the humour—but we can understand and love them all. Sterne achieves his effect by severely limiting the range of his view, leaving out all non-essentials, and concentrating almost entirely upon the significant details, tiny strokes of character, the little incidents and fleeting thoughts and fancies that can matter so much. In this his genius, which was absolutely original, anticipated not a little of what is characteristic of modern fiction. He had, too—if we overlook a few silly tricks—a style exquisitely suited to his purpose, a style that seems as easy and unconcerned as talk, and yet is most cunningly turned and cadenced, a perfection of art. Sterne had many imitators, all unsuccessful, the best of them being Henry Mackenzie (1745–1831), whose *Man of Feeling* is a delicate orgy of sentimentalism. But a more important tale than Mackenzie's, and one very different in matter and manner, appeared in the year that saw the first volume of *Tristram Shandy*. This was Johnson's *Rasselas*, which is neither a picture of manners nor a study in sentiment, but a moral fable, ponderous and gloomy but full of steady thought, the weight of which crushes the fiction. More important still was the story that appeared when *Tristram Shandy* was ending its course, in 1766—*The Vicar of Wakefield*, by Oliver Goldsmith (1728–1774). The tale itself is comparatively slight, and is told in the first person by the good Vicar himself, who has the simplicity and goodness of Fielding's Parson Adams. The plot is the familiar one of elopement on the one hand and abduction on the other, and is very badly put together. It is not the story but the people who matter, for there is all Goldsmith's happy humour and curious charm in his pictures of the Vicar and his family, the Primroses, who are all delightful and affectionate simpletons, whose ignorance of the world and innocent vanity lead them into all manner of absurdities. There is about this little tale, which soon became famous and found its way all over Europe, an atmosphere of happy innocence and affection, a kind of poetry of humorous domesticity; and the charm of Goldsmith's style and manner, " brightening everything he touched," remains with us; so that we can read of the Vicar and his misadventures to-day with nearly as much pleasure as our ancestors felt 150 years ago.

CHAPTER III

OUR task in this chapter is to press forward to where two peaks may be seen shining in the sky, each of them representing perfection in two very different forms of fiction. One of them is Sir Walter Scott (1771–1832), and the other is Jane Austen (1775–1817). When it is remembered that these two writers were born about the time that Goldsmith died, it will be seen that we have some distance to go. The way is strewn with names of novels and novelists, but we cannot stop to examine them. The most we can do is to consider the various kinds or schools of fiction that came into existence. The age, of course, was that of the so-called " Romantic Revival." People became interested in the past, especially in the Middle Ages. Sometimes this interest was purely historical.

39

Sometimes it was purely romantic, delighting in ruins, skeletons, ghosts, witches, mysterious monks, elixirs of life, whatever, in short, was capable of exciting wonder. The old ballads, legends, fairy-tales, became popular, and when the local supply failed, were imported from Germany. The public for fiction was growing rapidly, and its members, whose own lives were usually very uneventful, grew tired of moral satire and fine sentiment, and asked to be thrilled. At first, this new romantic fiction was the work of amused amateurs, such as Horace Walpole, who concocted a wild medieval legend in his *Castle of Otranto*, and the young millionaire, William Beckford, who created in *Vathek* a genuine Arabian Night. But very quickly this new manner in fiction became fashionable; the public liked it, and demanded more and more; so that it was not long before tales of wonder and terror poured into the bookshops and circulating libraries. The ordinary reader of that time became as great a connoisseur of ghosts and secret passages and moving statues as the ordinary reader of to-day is of missing jewels and finger-prints. Indeed, the novels of the " School of Terror," with which the names of such writers as Mrs. Radcliffe, Lewis, and Maturin are connected, may be aptly compared to the detective story of to-day. The best of these novelists, the three mentioned above, were not entirely without literary power, but, nevertheless, what was chiefly demanded of them was ingenuity and not imagination. If it is impossible to be thrilled any longer by the best of these tales, such as Mrs. Radcliffe's *Mysteries of Udolpho*, that is only because her devices have since been used over and over again.

Certain other writers, theorists like Godwin, daubed the jam of this ultra-romantic fiction round their philosophical pills. They combined a passion for the most barren and abstract social theorising, which settled all our affairs by the application of a few first principles, with an equal passion for all the absurdities of ultra-romantic story-telling,

2 *

for Rosicrucian meetings and elixirs of life and secret passages and blood-drinkers' burials. It is a strange combination; but both their theorising and their story-teller's trappings and tricks are alike in that both result from giving common sense a holiday and from refusing to look steadily at reality. Shelley and his wife, as writers of fiction, belonged to this school, which was admirably satirised by Peacock in his *Nightmare Abbey*, just as the more obvious Gothic-ruin-and-terror school was satirised by Jane Austen in *Northanger Abbey*. Many of these romantic tales were set in the past, chiefly in a fire-and-brimstone Middle Ages. This was something new. All the great eighteenth-century novels deal with their own times. But history itself had become popular; the old ballads and folk tales were collected and studied; there was a new interest in the past; thus the appearance of historical fiction, the kind of story that links up the fortunes of its chief character with some great events of the past, was inevitable. As Sir Walter Raleigh observed : " An interest in past history, a desire to revive in fiction the picturesque elements of bygone institutions and customs, were of the essence of the romantic revival." Many attempts were made to create what we now call the Historical Novel. They all failed because the writers either gave us the novel without the history, or the history without the novel. This kind of fiction demanded a special genius, an imagination that warmed to the task of penetrating the crust of mere fact, breaking through into the real living world of the past, and in addition the usual equipment of the good novelist of manners, a knowledge of character and so forth. That such a genius should have come out of Scotland is not surprising, for in no country is the historical imagination more lively. In 1814, Walter Scott, who was already popular as a romantic narrative poet, who had already done much editorial and critical work on the ballads and folk tales of his country, published, anonymously, his first novel, *Waverley*, and a new kind of fiction was born. Very soon the whole world was talking about the wonderful " Scotch Novels."

No novelist of his rank is more easy to criticise adversely than Scott. He makes a huge target. The neat story-tellers have complained that he is untidy; the passionate novelists have told us that he knew nothing about love; the philosophical novelists have condemned him for lack of ideas; the stylists have sneered at his clumsy prose; the historians have pointed out his anachronisms; the very schoolboys, condemned to study him when they might have been playing ball, have declared that he is dull. We can easily multiply such charges. His heroes are generally mere sticks, and his heroines so many walking gowns. Neither the height nor the depth of feeling is his. He cannot give us, as Bagehot said, the delineation of a soul. What then is left when all these charges (except that of the schoolboy, though even he is not without reason) are admitted ? The answer is easy—there is left a whole

wide world of enthralling event and living
people, the world into which we can enter
every time we pick up a novel by Scott.   To
deny his genius in fiction is only to condemn
yourself as one who holds some hopelessly
narrow view of the art.   The stir and bustle
of life, the march of event, the humour and
pathos and heroism in high places and low
places, the varied scene, the panorama of hill
and dale and crowded street, vital human
nature in almost all its phases—this is what
Scott gives us, pours out with the generosity
of a god.   His work is like a vast city, and
that is why it is so easy to criticise adversely.
One man goes to the city and denounces it
because he cannot find there a woman to fall
in love with, another because he cannot take
a degree at the university, another because
there are too many people in the streets and
too much noise for his weak nerves; but
what are these compared with the thousands
who have found delight there ?   Scott was
so exalted in his own time and immediately
afterwards, when his shadow fell across

Europe, that it soon became an amusing pastime of criticism to attack his reputation, to throw into relief every weakness and limitation. At the present time there are probably thousands and thousands of readers who have denied themselves the lasting pleasure of this great novelist's acquaintance, and take upon themselves to condemn a vast fabric of which they have at most seen only a few worn stones. Scott was an historical novelist, who brought his own kind of fiction nearer to perfection than any other writer before or since has succeeded in doing; but in order to appreciate his genius it is necessary to throw the emphasis not upon " historical " but upon " novelist." His best work is undoubtedly to be found in the stories of Scotland in the seventeenth and eighteenth centuries, and some of it, such as *The Antiquary*, takes little or no colouring from history. He could still have been a great novelist if he had never made use of a single historical fact or figure. (It is the common use of his later and weaker tales in schools—as a kind of supplement to the text-books—that has probably prejudiced innumerable readers against them.) He had a massive knowledge of human nature, particularly as it is seen in the ordinary hurly-burly of life, and the further gift, without which he could never have excelled in fiction, of abundant and life-like creation. The world of his fiction, in which comedy and tragedy jostle one another as they do in Shakespeare, is shaped by his own robust sense and coloured by his generous feelings and his eloquence; and it is one of the largest, manliest, noblest that the Novel can show us.

Meanwhile, another and very different kind of fiction was being perfected by Jane Austen. The Novel, in Scott's hands, broadened out to mirror a whole roaring world, great events, and crowds on the march. In Jane Austen's delicate hands it becomes a miniature, " on which I work with so fine a brush as produces little effect after much labour." There could not be a

sharper contrast between two novelists.
When Scott built up his world he laid hands
on almost everything but the tea-tables;
and it was out of tea-tables and other
domestic oddments that Jane Austen created
her own little world. It was the one she
knew intimately, and so she chose quite
deliberately to remain in it. She banished
from it nine-tenths of life, and gave us people
who never work or fight or die, or starve or
go crazy, a world in which a shower of rain
is an event, in which there are no wars nor
politics nor commerce nor furious passions
nor violent deaths. This she had to do in
order that her delicate and subtle comedy
might be played in peace. She made all her
characters cosy and comfortable in order
that they might feel at home, and talk away
and thus display themselves to us. What
she asks us to observe are the little egotisms
and absurdities of this life, and she knew very
well that we should care nothing about such
things unless we met them in an atmosphere
of leisure and comfort and security, round a

tea-table and not a camp-fire or a death-bed. She creates fiction out of material that might easily be the substance of a correspondence between two ladies living in the most retired parts of the country. Women had been writing novels steadily throughout the eighteenth century, but they had made little attempt to exploit characteristically feminine sides of life and points of view. Jane Austen was not, however, the first to do this, for she had one important predecessor in Fanny Burney (1752–1840), whose first and best novel, *Evelina*, has considerable merit. But in Jane Austen's six novels, *Northanger Abbey*, *Sense and Sensibility*, *Pride and Prejudice* (which contains the most sparkling comedy), *Mansfield Park*, *Emma* (perhaps the best as an all-round tale), and the exquisite *Persuasion*, what we might call domestic fiction instantly achieves something as near perfection as human frailty can conceive. They are the best examples in literature of the cool feminine outlook, unclouded by any passionate sympathies or desires, quite detached and terribly observant, surveying a very restricted field of manners and character through a microscope and never missing the slightest trait, the tiniest absurdity, the least affectation.   Jane Austen has been justly regarded as the most perfect artist in English fiction : what she sets out to do, that she does with what seems to be consummate ease.   She is entirely detached from her characters, like all great ironists, and she never seems to meddle with them, as some of the greatest men novelists do, and never obtrudes herself.   Her first novel, *Northanger Abbey*, was written when she was absurdly young, and yet her art in it is almost fully developed.   There is really little to choose between her early work and her later. Some critics have preferred the later work, and indeed it is more elaborately constructed and exquisitely turned, but on the other hand it lacks something of the sparkling irony of the earlier.   Grant her the scope she demanded, free her from the charge of not dealing with matters she never pretended to deal with, and she has fewer weaknesses than any novelist named in these pages.   No doubt many readers, accustomed by this time to violent and easy effects, are repelled by her cool formality and by the unusually narrow interests of her people, who are capable of talking for a month about an invitation to a ball; but such readers are only paying the penalty of a ruined palate for fine literature.   While her people are chatting and gossiping about the ball, their creator is coolly and exquisitely presenting her version of the perpetual human comedy, in which the reader of novels and the critic of them have their parts too.   To watch her making delicate stroke after stroke is a most delightful and engrossing pastime, one that will not leave even the keenest wits idle.   And few novelists " wear " better than she does. Her people amuse us more the third or fourth time we read about them than they do the first time.   " She has given us," said Macaulay, one of her most enthusiastic admirers, " a multitude of characters, all in a certain sense commonplace, such as we meet every day. Yet they are all as perfectly discriminated from each other as if they were the most eccentric of human beings." By the sheer enchantment of art, she transforms people who, if we met them in real life, would bore us to tears, into the most entertaining characters : Mr. Collins, Miss Bates, Mr. Woodhouse. She is not equally good with everybody : thus her young women are incomparably better than her young men, who are not falsely drawn, but are never seen against a masculine background; we feel that their creator does not know what they do or what they say to one another once they have left the ladies and the parlour. But her young women, Catherine Morland, Elizabeth Bennet, Emma Woodhouse, Anne Elliot, were easily the most life-like and attractive that fiction had so far offered. And some of their comic elders have never been surpassed.

The Novel was now in a very different

position. Its range had been extended in opposite directions. Scott had gone out, like one of his own Border raiders, and looted history itself. Jane Austen had stayed at home, and had shown that by making use of tiny scraps of the most commonplace material it was possible to produce the most delightful fiction. Moreover, the attitude towards the Novel had changed, for it was no longer regarded as an inferior form of literature, only fit for girls and idle young men or for serious adults determined for once to unbend their minds. Scott had created an immense public for fiction, a public drawn from all classes, and had opened a way for the serious professional novelist, though, in spite of the fortune he made out of his fiction, he thought of himself to the last as a poet and legal gentleman who happened to have stumbled on this trick of writing novels. Nevertheless, circumstances compelled him at times to regard himself as a professional writer of fiction, who had to work with one eye upon the taste of his public.   Not one of the least significant moments in the history of nineteenth-century English fiction was that when Scott agreed to alter (and spoil) the plot of *St. Ronan's Well*, at the request of his publisher, who believed that the public would be shocked by it.   The frankness of Fielding and the humorous licence of Sterne were no longer possible, not merely because manners themselves had changed, but also because the Novel had become a middle-class family entertainment.   The next three generations of novelists were condemned to an absurd reticence.   Life was much the same then as it had been before and has been since; the whole tragi-comedy of intimate sexual relations was being played as usual; but the novelist could not say so.   This fact should be borne in mind throughout the two chapters that follow.   It almost shut out one side of life from the Victorian novelist, to our loss; but its further effect was to make him concentrate more than he might have done on certain other sides of life, so that there was some gain, if only in variety. We have discovered since then that when we are all allowed to say what we please, we all tend to say the same thing.

CHAPTER IV

DICKENS AND THACKERAY

THE names now begin to multiply, and
with them the kinds of fiction. We can see
the Novel branching out in all directions.
Thus the kind that Scott had made so
popular was continued by two indefatigable
writers, G. P. R. James (1801–1860) and
William Harrison Ainsworth (1805–1882),
both of whom brought a great deal more
history and a great deal less knowledge of life
and men and women into fiction than Scott
did: they were both widely read and
admired at first, but before they had done
they merely succeeded in bringing the
historical novel into disrepute. Bulwer
Lytton (1803–1873), who did so many
things, began writing novels as early as 1825
and kept it up for nearly half a century,

during which time he contrived to produce whatever type of fiction, sentimental, sensational, historical, humorous-domestic, was fashionable at the moment. He had any amount of talent, and can still be read with pleasure (his *Strange Story* and *The Haunted and the Haunters* are really good), but there was always something rather slap-dash and insincere about him. He lacked that confidence in himself which distinguishes Disraeli, Lord Beaconsfield (1804–1881), who also began writing novels early (his first, *Vivian Grey*, was published in 1826), and after that brought them out at fairly long intervals during a life mainly devoted to politics. Disraeli is both difficult to classify and to estimate as a novelist. His political novels—and these are his best—are full of ideas and wit and good caricatures, if not characters, but they contain other elements, romantic, fantastic or mystical, that refuse to blend; and the result is a curious unreality : he creates a shifting sort of world that seems at one moment a scathing satire of political high life and at the next moment something that is more like an Arabian Night than any possible version of Victorian England; and he has a style that somehow turns all his gold into gilt and his marble into stucco, or when it does not do that, simply gives everything it touches an air of unreality. There is, however, capital entertainment in him : his very failings are amusing. Among the other novelists who had made their reputation before Dickens arrived were Captain Marryat (1792–1848), whose sea-stories, especially *Peter Simple* and *Mr. Midshipman Easy*, are excellent, hearty tales of adventure with some genuine humour in them; and Thomas Love Peacock (1785–1866), who wrote novels that are hardly stories at all, but magnificent satirical or farcical dialogues, ridiculing a great number of contemporary opinions, connected by passages of description written in very fine ironic prose, the whole producing an effect of intellectual high spirits that is unique in English literature.

In 1837 two reigns began, that of Queen Victoria and that of Mr. Pickwick. We have arrived at Charles Dickens (1812–1870). The literary history of Dickens is, briefly, that he began with the old, rambling, purely episodic tale of Smollett, an almost artless affair, and gradually tightened and elaborated his construction and went to work more and more deliberately and with greater art; but that as his technique improved the force of his native genius weakened. His later stories are better novels than the earlier ones, but they are not better Dickens. His early stories are extraordinarily crude, filled with the most preposterous melodrama—such as the Mulberry Hawk passages in *Nicholas Nickleby*—but nevertheless the fire of his genius burns more brightly in them. *Little Dorrit* is a far better piece of work, as a specimen of the novelist's craft, than *Martin Chuzzlewit*, which is simply like a vast improvisation, but there are far more transcendent things, things that nobody but Dickens could have written, in the earlier tale, and therefore we prefer it. There is, however, one period in his life when the craftsman is awake and alert, and the original inspiration has not yet weakened; and it was that period that gave us *David Copperfield*. But as soon as we compare him with other novelists and not with himself, he seems all of a piece, and the last page he wrote like the very first, so widely removed is he from any other writer, so completely original. " The Inimitable," he liked to call himself, and he was right. If ever a novelist gave us a world of his own, Dickens did. We have only to peep into it for a second or so to recognise it. It is essentially a fantastic world, at some remove from the one most of us know. The materials of which it is composed seem realistic enough; Dickens, who saw and remembered everything that came his way, crammed it full of facts and acute observation; here is no vague dreamland, but a place filled with sharply etched detail; yet it seems a very strange realm he shows us, situated somewhere between

Victorian England and Elfland. This is because of the very unusual quality of his imagination. He compels us to look through his eyes—his imagination being very intense and therefore compelling—and they are no ordinary eyes. They are the eyes of a man who never escaped or never was exiled from his childhood. Clutton-Brock pointed this out some years ago. Dickens' life, he tells us, " was not divided into periods of childhood, youth, and middle age; his experience was always of the same kind. People and things affected him to the last, just as they had affected him when he first began to take notice; and since there were no divisions in his own life, he took no account of such divisions in the lives of others. He says, somewhere, that feelings which we think serious in a man seem to us comical in a boy; but he himself reversed the process. Children are nearly always serious to him. It is men who seem to him absurd, when they conceal their childishness behind beards and large white waistcoats.

He loved those who, like himself, remained children all their lives; but the others seemed to him to be playing some kind of stupid game. . . ." This is well said. It explains why there is so much missing from his world, which has no place for so many concerns and people, from ideas to sexual passion, from philosophers to fine ladies. " It is remarkable," writes one of his best critics, Mr. Santayana, " in spite of his ardent simplicity and openness of heart, how insensible Dickens was to the greater themes of the human imagination—religion, science, politics, art. He was a waif himself, and utterly disinherited. . . . Perhaps, properly speaking, he had no *ideas* on any subject; what he had was a vast, sympathetic participation in the daily life of mankind." What entered into his imagination as a child is to be found in the world of his novels, and those things that could not enter remained for ever outside that world. Thus, negative criticism, dealing with nothing but weaknesses and limitations, can play such havoc

with Dickens that we are left wondering
what possible claim he can have to be considered a great novelist. His whole world
is fantastic and lop-sided and terribly incom-
plete.   Even if we ignore what it leaves out,
there is still much to be said against the
things that are included in it. His plotting
may be good plotting of its kind (Mr.
Arnold Bennett once said it was), but the
fact remains that it has long been tiresome to
us. His men and women never rise above
easy or bashful affection to the poetic passion
of love. His morality is an affair of melodramatic black and white. His people are
either good or bad; if good, they never have
a vicious impulse, and if bad, never a decent
one. His villains have no common stuff of
humanity in them : they are just bogeymen,
grotesque figures in a shadowgraph. His
deliberate pathos, when we can catch him
bringing out the handkerchiefs in readiness
for the flood of tears that will shortly follow,
can be simply sickening, an outrage. When
he is not working at his best, even his comic

characters become tedious mechanisms that merely go on repeating certain catch-words and gestures. We will mention no further weaknesses, though there are plenty of them. It is sufficient to say that no intelligent and fairly sensitive novel-reader, however great his (or her) enthusiasm for Dickens, can read any one of his novels—with the possible exception of *Pickwick*—from beginning to end without experiencing innumerable moments of tedium, discomfort, and even downright shame. And once we have come to know our Dickens, we do not, in actual fact, read him solidly, missing nothing; we do not hesitate to skip a good deal.

All these faults and limitations were pointed out long ago. It is not true to say that they do not matter, but it is certainly true to say—as literary history shows us— that they matter very little. The positive qualities, the virtues, of Dickens are so astounding and transcendent that adverse criticism can riddle him through and through and yet leave him comparatively unhurt.

His imagination is childish, and that is his weakness. But his imagination is also child-like, and there is his strength. He sees nothing dully and trivially. First and last he has the curiosity and zest and tearing energy of a boy just let loose from school. " What a face is his to meet in a drawing-room ! " cried Leigh Hunt. " It has the life and soul in it of fifty human beings." That life and soul he put into his books, in which even the very *things*, the houses and furniture, are alive, full of vitality and character. The common round of existence is transformed by that intense and child-like vision into something rich and strange, steeped in atmosphere, now dark and touched with a sinister magic, now bright with pity and kindness, now radiant with the most enchanting high spirits. It is not the story he tells, but the world he shows us that fills us with delight. We do not care what happens there; we only ask to remain there. He introduces us to characters whose talk and antics are so gloriously diverting that these

3

characters exist in their own right; if they have little or nothing to do with the plot, then so much the worse for the plot; we do not care. These characters—Old Weller, Mr. Bumble, Vincent Crummles, Dick Swiveller, Mr. Pecksniff, the immortal Micawbers, and all the rest—have been called caricatures, but this is to misunderstand both them and their creator. Literature is full of caricatures, but it is not full of Dickens' characters, who are indeed a special creation, the inhabitants of a world other than this. Perhaps they never seem to us human beings, yet they move and breathe and have a colossal vitality of their own. The great absurd ones are entirely compact of absurdity, and there is no ordinary human stuff in them; they would be just as funny, we feel, on their death-beds. It is not true, however, to say that we have never met people at all like them; we have only to return in memory to our childhood and think of the odd adults we knew then, the comic friend of the family, a droll milkman or butcher,

to discover the outlines of Dickens' characters.   It would have been impossible then
for us to have imagined that these curious
people we knew could ever be anything but
funny; we saw them as a queer assemblage
of tricks of voice and gesture, as creatures
quite different from ourselves; and this is
precisely how Dickens saw his characters.
Dickens could turn off his sympathy, which
would have led him to identify himself with
these people, just as a child turns off its
sympathy from the strange adults whose
lives it cannot penetrate, and that therefore
seem meaningless.   That is the secret of his
satiric method of dealing with officials and
narrow professional men, fashionable people,
and big-wigs generally; as Clutton-Brock
has pointed out: " Everyone who fell into
routine, who seemed to act inexpressively
and with no sense of the fun of life, was
turned by him into a marionette."   On the
other hand, his sympathy, where it came into
play, was intense; that " life and soul of
fifty human beings " goes out to meet and

welcome the fun of life, whatever is warm
and friendly in human relations. His own
childhood, which had in part been that of a
waif and a drudge, for whom society does
nothing and a few generous souls everything, left its mark upon his mind : indeed,
as we have seen, he never really left it. He
became the friend and the champion of the
poor and the simple. His novels are like the
gigantic day-dreams of the little outcast in
the blacking factory : the cruel adults are all
severely punished; the cold sneering people
are mocked and buffeted; but all the
friendly and lovable souls are generously
entertained, and at last the fires and lamps
are lighted, the curtains drawn to hide the
dark streets, the tables set with food and
drink, and all the good people are happy.
No other novelist deals so largely with
happiness itself; some of his passages
remind us of the wonderful birthday parties
of our childhood; and it is significant that
his most characteristic tales show us a world
that is beyond time and change, with

characters, like gods or fairies, who never grow any older and who are always the same. Dickens frequently wrote with what we now call " a purpose," to bring into the limelight of his satire certain matters that might be remedied, it might be Yorkshire schools or workhouses or Chancery proceedings, and so forth, and he was able to call attention to various abuses. But too much has been made of this. We do not read him now for his social reform, and neither did our grand-fathers. He was only successful as a social reformer because he commanded a large audience, but he did not command that audience as a social reformer. He may have unmade Dotheboys Hall, but Dotheboys Hall did not make him. Other novelists of the time, as we shall see, attacked various abuses with as much vigour and more truth to fact than Dickens did, but their reputations do not keep step with his. Dickens the social reformer is dead now, unlike the essential Dickens, mocking at whatever is mechanical and cold, and for ever quickening to any warmth of heart, bringing a whole fantastic and genial world to vivid life, sharing the laughter and tears of vast multitudes of the poor and simple; Dickens the creator, whose great comic figures abide in our minds like gods and fairies, whose best moments are not merely like life but are better than life : this is the Dickens who will not die for many a year. He seems in so many ways to be very English, and indeed very Victorian; but there is something universal in his appeal; his genius has conquered many countries, and every generation discovers it afresh; wherever there is pity and laughter he can go in triumph. " The good, the gentle, high-gifted, ever-friendly, noble Dickens," Carlyle called him; and whole populations have caught up and resounded the praise.

It is a natural and easy step from Dickens to the great contemporary with whom it was once the fashion to compare and contrast him, William Makepeace Thackeray (1811–1863). Fortunately it is no longer necessary to praise one at the expense of the other. Something must be said about Thackeray's life. He was the child of Anglo-Indian parents, and was sent to England when he was very young to go to school, where he was lonely and rather unhappy. His career at Cambridge was very short, and anything but successful. He inherited a comfortable fortune, but was unlucky enough to lose it, through bad investments and dabbling in publishing. Then he turned to art (he afterwards illustrated some of his own novels), but did not succeed in earning a living. He became a contributor, first of reviews and burlesques, and later of tales, to magazines, but for years hovered on the brink of failure, until at last *Vanity Fair* brought him success in his late thirties. Meanwhile, his domestic life had been tragic, for his young wife broke down in health very early and finally lost her reason. Success, money, friendships, welcome as they were, came too late. He was a very affectionate man; far more the domestic-and-fireside character than Dickens

himself, and he had no real home, only a
club.   His early experiences, his own failure
and folly, and other men's roguery, had not
soured him, but they had hurt him; and the
tragedy of his marriage turned the hurt into
a wound.   He was no philosopher, not a
thinker, but a man of quick observation and
deep feeling; he could not think away the
evil, could not even grapple with it; he could
only wince and secretly probe his wounds.
Life began by hurting him, and thereafter
he goes wincing.   In his early work you can
find him retorting savagely to life; but in
his later work there is only a great melancholy.   He is for ever writing in the mood
of *Ecclesiastes* : " Vanity of vanities," saith
the Preacher.   There is a strain of weakness
running through all his work.   People in his
own day called him a cynic, and since then
he has been called a snob (whose delight it
was to hunt down snobs) and a sentimentalist.
He probably was something of a snob,
though the truth is—as " Q " has pointed
out—he did not really know his England;

he knew, no one better, the world between
Kensington and Cornhill, the big houses,
the clubs, the newspaper offices, the taverns,
but he did not know the English life that
Trollope shows us, and never understood it.
We must, however, go behind this to discover his great weakness as a novelist.
What is wrong with Thackeray is that his
thought lags far behind his feelings; his
is the manner and the mood of the philosophical novelist, but he has no philosophy;
he is a thousand times more sensitive than
the ordinary Victorian clubman, but unfortunately his mental outlook, his ideas, are
only those of the ordinary Victorian clubman; he is like some great eager talker who
suddenly finds himself in a drawing-room in
which such subjects as religion, politics, art,
and love are tabooed; he seems to be for
ever cracking nuts with a sledge-hammer.
The small snob is the legitimate prey of some
easy, light-hearted satirist and not of this
huge, melancholy man, who spends far too
much of his time sneering in the drawing-

3 *

room or poking about in the servants' hall. Thackeray is a far greater writer than Trollope, but he is a far more unsatisfactory novelist : the Trollope novel perfectly expresses Trollope, but the Thackeray novel does not really express Thackeray, who knows all the time that he has picked up an instrument with too small a compass. Hence his frequent weariness and disdainful shrugging, his trick of thrusting " his puppets " to one side; hence, too, our own frequent dissatisfaction and irritation when we are reading him, our feeling that it is all too cramped and stuffy.

When we have said this, we have said the worst. We have lately become more appreciative of Thackeray's vices than of his virtues, if only because the later history of the novel has thrown into relief his insufficiency but has done little, on the other hand, to make us more sensitive to his excellencies. These are incomparable in English fiction. On his own ground he cannot be beaten. He was a hasty and hand-to-mouth writer,

always improvising and hardly ever con-
structing a novel, but he has a miraculous
style, for ever running easily on, but con-
triving always to find the appropriate movement and music for every possible mood.
It is as easy as talk and yet as enchanting as a
good sonata.   Indeed, all his novels, huge
as they are, seem to be talked at us; they are
not presented directly and dramatically;
they are like gigantic essays (Thackeray was
a born essayist); the writer seems to be
searching his memory, peering through its
haze at distant scenes and figures, and
gradually clarifying his vision of things past.
He has been well called the novelist of
memory.   " Thackeray is everybody's past,"
Mr. Chesterton once wrote, " is everybody's
youth.   Forgotten friends flit about the
passages of dreamy colleges and unremem-
bered clubs; we hear fragments of unfinished conversations, we see faces without
names for an instant, fixed for ever in one
trivial grimace : we smell the strong smell
of social cliques now quite incongruous to

us; and there stir in all the little rooms at once the hundred ghosts of oneself." He combines a wide panoramic vision of the social scene with a few moments of great drama; he lights up half a hundred characters for us and keeps them all in motion; he bathes everything in atmosphere and yet never sacrifices the effect of ordinary reality; he can always keep Time ticking away, flowing on, unlike most novelists, who must either get outside it altogether or can only move it forward in big jerks. Much could be said in praise of his shrewd observation, his delightful humour and unforced pathos; more could be said of his character-drawing, for he has given us a wonderful gallery— Becky Sharp, Major Pendennis, Esmond, Beatrix (both as a young beauty and as a hard old woman), Colonel Newcome, and a host of others; but what is unique in him, and must always bring readers back to him, is his amazingly deft and subtle manipulation of the whole wide scene of the social life he is dealing with, whether it is the Victorian

London of the fashionable houses and clubs and the taverns in *Pendennis* or *The Newcomes*, or the Bloomsbury of the Waterloo period in his masterpiece, *Vanity Fair*, or the early eighteenth-century England of his other and perhaps even greater masterpiece, *Esmond*, which still remains one of the glories of English fiction.

CHAPTER V

THE state of fiction in the middle of the nineteenth century can be suggested by the title of one of its novels, *Yeast*. The author of that novel, Kingsley, wished to call attention to the social ferment. Fiction itself was also fermenting. Every year brought more novel readers and therefore more novels. There were innumerable circulating libraries ready to welcome novels in the familiar three-volume form. Certain of the more popular novelists first published their work in fortnightly and monthly parts, illustrated by artists like Cruikshank and Leech and " Phiz," who had a large following themselves. Both Dickens and Thackeray did this, and it partly explains why their tales were so long and rambling and badly constructed. So, too, did

Charles Lever (1806–1875), whose gigantic and artless chronicles of high jinks in military life were extremely popular.   With the railways came the railway bookstall, which soon called into existence a special one-volume cheap edition of the novel that kept quite a number of writers busy.   The various periodicals and magazines that appeared published serial stories, and not a few of the most famous novels of the period came out first in this way.   Now that it was so popular, the Novel became like a kind of newspaper, reflecting in various forms all the different interests of the time : society women wrote society novels; soldiers, such as James Grant, wrote military novels; hunting men like Surtees and Whyte-Melville wrote hunting novels; and even a philological vagabond like George Borrow turned his queer experiences to good use in volumes that are, perhaps, more like novels than they are like anything else.   The output of fiction grew apace, and industrious women novelists, such as Mrs. Oliphant and Charlotte Yonge (both of them possessed of talent, which they sadly over-worked), each produced scores and scores of tales. But the popularity of the Novel meant more than this. It offered any and every kind of writer a possible large audience, and it was soon seen to be so elastic in form that it could be made to serve all manner of interests.

Thus we discover the young Rector of Eversley, Charles Kingsley (1819–1875), turning to fiction, in *Yeast*, not so much because he wants to tell a tale, to create character, to build up a world of his own, but because he is perturbed at the state of society, and especially the situation of the agricultural labourers. He sees that it is possible in fiction to give readers such a picture of contemporary life as will almost compel them to draw certain conclusions. He makes the Novel frankly topical and argumentative. This he continued to do, and even his historical romance, *Westward Ho!* is something of a Protestant tract, though it is a good many other things beside. The Forties were times of great distress; many reforms were urgently needed; industry was at its blackest and foulest, and innumerable revelations were made concerning its slavery; and for the following twenty or thirty years there were unusually strong humanitarian impulses at work in literature. Small wonder that the Novel came to have a direct political purpose, shaped its fable to throw into relief some terrible social evil. Dickens himself led the way, and some of the others who followed —Disraeli, Charles Reade, Kingsley, Mrs. Gaskell—were, perhaps, more effective than he was. We, the novel-readers of posterity, must necessarily be heartless about this matter. A novel may have worked kindly marvels in its day, may have stirred the whole nation to a generous indignation and have freed a host of children from the factory, but if we cannot enjoy such a novel, we cannot enjoy it : as a social document it may live, but as a work of art it is dead. And we must not be surprised if so many of these novels with a purpose, dictated as they were by the noblest feelings, seem poor faded stuff now. They were frequently written with an eye to an immediate effect, and the warm partisan, hoping to enlist opinion on his side, is rarely in a fit state to create a work of art. The political-social novel of the mid-century was undoubtedly good for the nation, but it was not, from our point of view, very good for fiction. Look for the weakest work of the novelists of the period (beginning with Dickens' *Hard Times*), and then search that work for its poorest chapters, and you will generally discover that you have made your way to what was capital social propaganda. And it is frequently only what the novelist himself (or herself) imagined to be mere trimming that is keeping the tale from oblivion.

The Novel, then, was laying hold of all manner of new material. It was more than usually successful in 1847, for in that year *Jane Eyre* was published, the first and best novel of Charlotte Brontë (1816–1855). It was a great success, and deservedly, because

it did represent something new in fiction.
If Jane Austen (whom Charlotte Brontë
despised) stands for the cool, detached
feminine point of view, that of the woman
who asks nothing for herself, but is content
to look on and smile, Charlotte Brontë
represents the passionate feminine point of
view, that of the woman who demands from
life the full satisfaction of her desires and
dreams.   She wrote directly out of her own
experience, and said, as frankly as she could,
what was in her mind.   All her three novels,
Jane Eyre, *Shirley*, and *Villette*, are strongly
autobiographical.   Jane Eyre is herself,
charity schoolgirl and governess, simply
thrust into a sensational story; Shirley is a
portrait of her sister Emily, and the other
characters in the book are her Haworth
acquaintances; Lucy Snowe is herself again,
this time at M. Heger's *pensionnat* at Brussels,
and M. Paul Emanuel is a likeness of M.
Heger.   She recorded and confessed rather
than created, like many women novelists since
her day.   Outside her own rather narrow

experience she is very weak indeed; the intense reality of her best chapters only throws into relief the poor theatricality of her worst.   Thus her Mr. Rochester (the father of so many strong brutal heroes) is an obvious fake: he is simply—in Leslie Stephen's phrase—the personification of a true woman's longing for a strong master.   The fact that she has little knowledge of the world and less humour would not tell against her if she had been able to keep her work in her one key, if she had limited herself as severely to what she could make completely her own, as Jane Austen did; but as it is she shows us no such perfect fusion and harmony.   That is why she does not keep her place as Jane Austen keeps hers.   Huge chunks of her work—for example, nearly all of *Jane Eyre* after the interrupted wedding—have, as it were, gone stale; as we read them we do not think about life, but about the attitudes of the Forties.   But she brought into fiction the thrilling if sometimes strident voice of passionate and romantic womanhood.   She also brought into it a really poetic sense of atmosphere; her people move against a background of real wind and rain and snow, of black hills and blacker night. In this matter, however, she is the inferior of her sister Emily (1818–1848), a more intense and unified creature and a real poet, whose solitary tale, *Wuthering Heights*, is not so much a novel as a tragic prose poem on the one hand and sheer nightmare on the other. It is as crazy as the maddest Elizabethan tragedy, and its people are the same inhuman monsters of will, but nevertheless this wild vision of the moors is a more perfect work of art than any of Charlotte's novels. The whole Brontë family, a strangely tragic group, have long been the subjects of a kind of cult, and it is doubtful if now there are not more people interested in Charlotte as a member of that group, as a figure, than there are devoted and constant readers of her fiction.

It is an easy step from the Brontës to their biographer, Mrs. Gaskell (1810–1865), perhaps the most gracious figure in this chronicle.

She had neither Jane Austen's perfection of art nor the Brontës' flashes of genius, and there is no one work of hers that seems to us as good as she could make it or that even completely represents her. Her most famous book is, of course, *Cranford*, that idyllic and humorous picture of village life, but it is a series of sketches (and appeared as such in Dickens' paper, *Household Words*) rather than a novel. A good deal of her life, a very full, useful, and happy life, was passed in Manchester, and she had a better acquaintance with the evils of the mid-century industrialism than any other novelist of the time. She made use of her knowledge in more than one novel, and especially in *Mary Barton*, which may be said to bring a whole new class of people into fiction, and *North and South*, which is the first novel to exhibit the contrast between the two Englands, the manufacturing North and the rural South. But she did not confine herself to any particular type of novel. *Sylvia's Lovers* and the unfinished but substantial *Wives and Daughters* are domestic comedies of middle-class life not unlike those of Jane Austen, though with a broader sweep and not so delicately finished. *Cousin Phillis*, a long short story rather than a novel, and perhaps her best piece of writing, is an exquisite pastel of rural England. With a little more sheer creative power, unifying her work and giving her character-drawing a sharper edge, she would have been the greatest woman novelist we have had. As it is, she has an extraordinarily wide range, a fine balance of sense and sensibility, and, what is more important, perhaps, real personal charm. " It seems to me," wrote " Q " of her work, " elementally of the best literary breeding, so urbane it is, so disposedly truthful; so much of the world, quizzing it; so well aware, all the while, of another." Mrs. Gaskell is one of those writers (they all have charm) about whom no fuss is made, who do not become cults, but whom people go on reading and delighting in more and more, whose names are still living when some other and apparently

greater names are really dead, nothing but
vast ruined mansions. It would, perhaps, not
be fair to say that the imposing structure of
George Eliot (Mary Ann Evans, 1819–1880)
is actually a ruin, but it is certain that not
many lights are now to be seen in the win-
dows. During the last ten years of her life
(though her best work was produced much
earlier) she was regarded as the greatest
English novelist then living; but there are
very few people now who would be ready
to agree with the verdict. But we need not
be surprised at it. The early death of
Thackeray and the still earlier death of
Charlotte Brontë had left a wide gap to be
filled, and she contrived for a time to fill it
and to do something more. She destroyed
the last remnant of that once great army of
" serious readers " who regarded the Novel
as a mere entertainment. She introduced
fiction into an atmosphere of prayers and
fasting and high and solemn endeavour.
There are two women at work in George
Eliot. The first is the shrewd and humorous

girl who spent her years among typical
country and provincial people, and was
possessed of unusual powers of observation
and memory.   The second is the laborious
and sensitive woman who was assistant-
editor of the *Westminster Review*, the rational-
ist, the scholar, solemnly devoted to a bleak
culture and very typical of her period, who
asks us " to do without opium and live
through all our pain."   The history of her
career as a novelist may be summed up by
saying that the first George Eliot was
gradually ousted by the second.   Her early
work, *The Scenes of Clerical Life*, *Adam Bede*,
The Mill on the Floss, and *Silas Marner*, is filled
with scenes and personages that are amazingly
life-like, unforced in both their humour and
pathos.   In them something has been done
once and for all.   But even in these stories,
with the exception of the first, there is something at fault in her handling of the main
themes and characters.   Her later work,
Romola (an historical tale), *Felix Holt the
Radical*, *Middlemarch*, *Daniel Deronda*, has

immense labour in it and a more subtle psychology, but it is greatly inferior to the earlier. The life that gleamed before has gone, has disappeared with that girl who once lived in the Midlands. Her power as a novelist had nothing whatever to do with the ceaseless mental activities of her middle life, her rationalism and languages and sciences and history, though these studies certainly enriched that "large intelligence" which Swinburne praised in her work. It came, that power, from the memories of her girlhood, when she had missed nothing of the life about her. Her strength lay in her extraordinary faculty for close and accurate observation, and if we add to this that large intelligence mentioned above and an almost painful conscientiousness, we arrive at a formidable total. But she had very little of that quality we can only call creative imagination ; her fine and laborious mind could not catch fire ; where she is not quickened by memory, she is not quickened at all ; she cannot give life where life has never been ; she dissects her characters like a surgeon instead of setting them in motion like a god. The pure artist in her, the poet, the maker, was never very strong and died young. Her famous remark about learning to do without opium is a fine stoical utterance, but it does not suggest a mind that was at its happiest in sheer creation. Art thrives on a little opium.

Charles Reade (1814–1884) has already been mentioned. He was the most thorough-going of all the mid-Victorian novelists who wrote stories round various social abuses. *It's Never Too Late to Mend* fastens upon the prison system, *Hard Cash* upon the evils of private lunatic asylums, *Foul Play* upon the danger of overloaded ships and kindred subjects, and so on and so forth. He was the first—and in England certainly the most laborious—of the " document " novelists, who do not begin their stories until they are surrounded by notebooks and newspaper cuttings full of facts bearing on the kind of life they are about to describe. Reade's study was crammed with files and ledgers, all elaborately indexed, and he made great play with his knowledge of the most minute facts. Ironically enough, however, his other interest was the theatre, the very melodramatic theatre of that period ; he wrote a good many plays and preferred them to his novels, with the result that a passion for purely theatrical situations, a melodramatic habit of mind, was for ever leading him astray. His notebooks would bring him as close to the ordinary facts of life as a good reporter is, but the next moment his playbooks would lure him into being outrageously theatrical. He is, perhaps, the most unequal story-teller of his time. An eccentric, hot-tempered man, always quarrelling with somebody or something, he was amazingly uncritical; and in addition there is something rather repelling about his coarse and unbalanced mind. But he had certainly one gift that is now all too rare, a superb gift of narration. When his imagination has really caught fire and a great scene is to hand, he is as compelling as a cavalry charge, and if novelists were to be judged by a few extracts, he would seem one of the great geniuses of the century. This narrative power can be discovered in his stories with a purpose, and particularly in *It's Never Too Late to Mend*, but it is found at its best in his historical novel, *The Cloister and the Hearth*, a huge, crowded, and vividly coloured tale of the fifteenth century. It is too long and there are dull patches, but one or two scenes in it rise to an epic splendour. Nothing so magnificent can be found in the work of his fellow-novelist-melodramatist, Wilkie Collins (1824–1889). Collins is sometimes described as a lesser or imitation Dickens (they were great friends), but this is misleading. The thing that is least important in Dickens, the mechanical plot, is almost the whole of Collins, who might be said to be the grandfather of all our present writers of detective or mystery tales. His favourite device is to make nearly every character a narrator in turn, and his stories are like elaborate jigsaw puzzles.

This device enables him to keep the reader in suspense, but as most of these narrators are not very interesting in themselves and do not always keep strictly to the matter in hand, they are apt to be tedious; and Collins would probably have had more readers to-day if he had not introduced into his tales so many unnecessary housekeepers and lawyers to give evidence. His purely literary value is small, though some of his rogues, notably Count Fosco in *The Woman in White*, are amusing. But his ingenuity is amazing, as those who begin *The Moonstone* will find to their cost; and in addition he has at times a command, surprising in such a robust craftsman, of sinister and eerie effects. One or two scenes in *The Woman in White* and *Armadale* are like bad dreams, and are far more subtly horrible than anything, for example, in Poe's tales.

To leave Wilkie Collins for Anthony Trollope (1815–1882) is to move from gaslight into daylight. Trollope is a very surprising figure. To begin with, he was not strictly a professional writer at all; he was a Post Office official who only wrote in his spare time, but he was at once so methodical and fluent that he produced a very large number of novels and made a fortune out of them. Again, his limitations both as a man and an artist are very numerous and very obvious, and only his most fervent admirers would deny that out of his fifty novels at least thirty-five are hardly worth reading. Yet at the present time his reputation, unlike the reputations of so many of his contemporaries, is actually growing, and he is, perhaps, the only Victorian novelist who has been over-praised of late years. His best work is to be found in what is known as the *Barsetshire* series, six novels that deal with the society of a small cathedral city and the surrounding countryside, and especially with the clergy of the neighbourhood. The secret of Trollope is there in the very name of this county he has mapped out for us. Novelists are always inventing counties, Loamshires and the like, but they rarely succeed in making us believe even in their names. But " Barsetshire " is so convincing that we can imagine an American visitor travelling round the country looking for it. That is Trollope's touch. His better novels have some most amusing characters in them (his Mrs. Proudie is a great figure) and contain some entertaining intrigues, but their real strength lies, as it were, in their texture. They are extraordinarily real; we may believe that there are all manner of things in Barsetshire that Trollope does not understand and therefore cannot tell us about; but, on the other hand, we cannot help believing in Barsetshire itself. We may think it a very dull place— and sometimes it is—but we are convinced that it is there, and that we have only to pick up *Barchester Towers* or *The Last Chronicle of Barset* (and these two are the best) to be back in the district again. Trollope was a rather coarse and hearty fellow, apt to be insensitive both in his life and his literature, but he had taken up and down the country, into manor-houses and inn parlours (for his Post Office work turned him into a great traveller, and he was fond of company), a mind that stored away images of life that may have been rough but were unusually faithful, free from the distortions that a more sensitive mind might have given them. What he undertakes to write about, he knows about, and though he is for ever breaking off from his story to point out that he is only amusing you and himself, and that all is fiction (a trick that infuriated Henry James), he is as unsuccessful in persuading us that his narrative is unreal, a mere dream, as most novelists are unsuccessful in persuading us that their narratives are anything else. One kind of fiction, the novel of manners, aiming at a faithful picture of a given society at a given time, he brought as near to perfection as any man has brought it.

Trollope's death brings us to the Eighties,

4

and there has accumulated a whole host of minor novelists who have not been mentioned. Chief among these are George Macdonald, a Highland Scot, who left the ministry for literature and wrote a large number of novels and fairy tales (the best is *Phantastes*) that are full of defects, but have a fine brooding imagination in them; Joseph Henry Shorthouse, whose first book, a kind of High Church historical romance called *John Inglesant*, is an original achievement; Richard Doddridge Blackmore, whose historical tale, *Lorna Doone*, has been immensely popular, and whose work in general has any number of scattered virtues, but suffers from the defect of seeming " made " rather than created; William Hale White, who called himself " Mark Rutherford " and wrote some pieces of autobiographical fiction, notably *The Revolution in Tanner's Lane*, that have an introspective quality which anticipates a good deal of later fiction; William Black, a pleasant, easy romancer; and, among a multitude of women, the astonishing creature known as " Ouida," who really succeeded in creating a whole world of her own, and whose goodness and badness are both equally exhilarating. At the beginning of this chapter we noticed that the Novel had begun to reflect a variety of interests, that sporting and society and military and other kinds of fiction had begun to make their appearance. Now, at the end of the period, we can see that another and more subtle sort of specialisation had made its way into fiction. We find novelists abandoning the attempt to mirror in their art the whole life of man. One will concentrate upon his adventures in love; another upon his religious difficulties; another upon social abuses ; and so forth : the deliberately fasten upon sections of the world, a part of life. With the next two novelists, George Meredith (1828–1909) and Thomas Hardy (1840–1928), who are the subjects of the chapter that follows, we return to the old broad sweep, we see the Novel expanding again. But there is a difference. Fiction in their hands takes a new turn, or, to be exact, several new turns. The first and most important is that it is used quite definitely as the vehicle of a philosophy of life. We arrive at the philosophical novel.

CHAPTER VI

MEREDITH brought to fiction a mind that seems unfitted for it. He was a lyrical poet and he was a philosopher, though not, of course, a systematic one. He could express moods of romantic ecstasy, and he could embody profound truths in witty epigrammatic phrases. As a writer pure and simple, he was most amply gifted, and he catches the eye as a man of genius. But he lacked a good many qualities, and these happen to be the very qualities we associate with the novelist. Thus there could be no greater contrast to Meredith than that born novelist, Trollope, with his faithful observation, his easily directed sympathies, his sure knowledge of the social scene, his steady conduct of a narrative. Meredith had none of these things, and his fiction exhibits—sometimes painfully—the lack of them. He is a very bad narrator, never moving steadily forward, but always jumping from scene to scene; many of his situations and his people—chiefly the secondary characters—are unconvincing, absurd; the world he reveals is clearly not this world, and there is about it something empty, brittle, abstract; no novels of the century seem to have less to do with the multitude of common facts, the business and bustle of ordinary life, and even with time and place. He makes not the slightest attempt to make things solid and familiar, to give us the illusion of common reality that is the triumph of such a novelist as Trollope. His aim seems to be to bewilder and bedazzle the reader. His style will do anything but make a plain statement; it indulges in the most extraordinary antics; and in its riot of strained metaphor and tortured wit all sense is sometimes lost. It seems incredible that such a writer, who might be admirable occasionally in a lyrical flight or a witty essay, should ever have attempted fiction. But Meredith not only attempted it, but succeeded in it. All the defects we have mentioned may be found in his novels, together with some others, and the total list is a formidable one, so that we need not be surprised if a great many people, who cannot enjoy his peculiar virtues, should be unable to read him with any pleasure. He remains, however, a great if somewhat lop-sided novelist.

Had Meredith tried to write the sort of fiction his contemporaries were writing, he would have remained a mere eccentric. He touched greatness because he invented, to suit his peculiar powers, a new kind of novel. It might be described as romantic comedy. His very sophisticated and critical intelligence had long found pleasure in intellectual comedy, of the type we associate with Molière, in which the follies and hypocrisies of men are shown in a very strong, clear light. On the other hand, the poet in him delighted in the sweep and passion of romantic narrative, and, above all, in the moments of ecstasy when the whole world seems bathed in strange light and colour, earth enchanted. The Meredith novel is a combination of these two forms, comedy and highly romantic narrative. In all his most characteristic stories the action is a very complicated comedy, in which egoists, self-deceivers, and self-coddlers are the victims. At times, when the author cannot restrain his soaring high spirits, the comedy turns into farce, the satire into humour, as it does when that glorious creature, Richmond Roy, dominates the scene in *Harry Richmond*. But in these same stories there is something besides satire and irony, wit or humour ; there are moments of pure romance, when the author, waving aside the comic spirit, rises to a lyrical ecstasy that has never been bettered by any novelist before or since. The scene of the meeting of the two young lovers in *The Ordeal of Richard Feverel* is one of the supreme romantic passages in English fiction. In his best work there is a mingling of poetry and wit that makes it unusually exhilarating. Meredith was a bad story-teller because he only cared for the great scene and did not trouble himself overmuch as to how he arrived at it, but once he has the great scene to hand he is superb, lavishing the rich stores of his mind on us. And he was one of the first—just as he can be one of the best—of what are called the "subjective" novelists, those who deal so largely in thoughts and impressions, living inside the minds of their characters. This method can easily be very tedious, but Meredith is never tedious. He penetrates into the mind of a character with a quick flash of light, and sometimes throws out a scene completely coloured and shaped by the thought and emotion of the chief personage involved in it, so that we, too, actually live in the scene. Another great gain in his fiction is his treatment of women and love. There is some good philosophy about women and love throughout his work, but in his best novels there is something better—namely, some

4 *

great women characters and some great love
scenes.   Meredith's heroines, especially Clara
in *The Egoist* and Nataly in *One of Our Conquerors*, are, perhaps, his greatest triumphs
in the creation of character; they are worlds
away from the sentimentalised dolls of most
Victorian fiction.   These women of his are
so successful because they are definite
individualities, playing their part, a very
important one, in his comedy, and are yet
highly poetical figures, for ever suggesting
glamorous beauty.   The whole treatment of
sexual relations is at once more frank and yet
more truly romantic in Meredith's novels
than it had been in any others of the century.
He has been called, not unjustly, the first of
the modern novelists.   His weaknesses cannot be disregarded, for not only are his
novels badly told and constructed, but there
is in them a lack of affection and more than a
hint of priggishness, snobbery, and affectation; but in the best of his work, throughout *The Egoist* (undoubtedly one of the great
novels of English literature), and in the

finest scenes in *Richard Feverel, Beauchamp's Career, Harry Richmond,* and *One of Our Conquerors,* there is triumphant genius.

Meredith and Hardy are not in complete contrast—as so many people have said they are—because they are both poet-philosophers who have created fiction on the grand scale. But in certain matters they are in very sharp contrast. Meredith is a fighting optimist, Hardy a dour but pitiful pessimist. Meredith's concern in fiction is with ultra-sophisticated persons, with the comedy of man in society, whereas Hardy's is with very simple people, with the tragedy of man and Nature. " The conduct of the upper classes," Hardy once wrote, " is screened by conventions, and thus the real character is not easily seen ; if it is seen, it must be portrayed subjectively ; whereas in the lower walks, conduct is a direct expression of the inner life ; and thus character can be directly portrayed through the act." So he elected to deal with simple people, and it is when he leaves them and tries to handle sophisti-

cated and educated persons that he is at his
weakest.   He selected one tract of countryside, far removed from large towns and
industrialism, as the scene of his operations.
His own native county of Dorset became the
Wessex of his novels.   Thus he becomes the
first—as he is easily the greatest—of what
have been called " regional " novelists.   But
he differs from later and smaller novelists
who have confined themselves to one territory in that the main interest of his work has
nothing whatever to do with this " regional
interest."   He does not ask us to read his
novels because they exploit, in travel-book
or guide-book fashion, the scenery and quaint
customs of Dorset.   He simply makes use
of the countryside he knows best.   But he
makes use of it in a new way.   The woods
and heaths and fields of his Wessex do not
supply him merely with so much scenery
against which his characters move, as they
would have done to an earlier novelist.
There are two strains in Hardy, and both of
them affected his treatment of the natural

scene. He is deeply and broodingly poetical, so that he can look at nothing long, though it is only a stick or a stone, without bringing it to life. Nature herself is one of the characters in his best novels : the woods in *The Woodlanders*, Egdon Heath in *The Return of the Native ;* these become living presences in the fiction. No other novelist is his equal in thus suggesting the vast brooding life of the earth itself. At his best he makes the natural background of other novelists seem like daubed canvas. But there is another strain in him that makes his approach different, for he brings to fiction the scientific temper of his time, which is that of Darwin and the great biologists. His Wessex is the *special environment* of his characters, whose development could not be understood without reference to it. Where former novelists saw their characters moving, as it were, before a painted wall, he sees them in their environment like fish swimming in a tank. The woods and heaths of Wessex, the clouds and stars and rain, its prejudices and customs,

and even its market prices, the whole atmosphere of the time and place, are the tank, and
the souls of his characters are the fish.   And
this scientific approach of his, inspired (if the
term is allowed) by a view of the universe
that is beginning now to remind us of some
clumsy old machine, leads him in a contrary
direction, and we discover him robbing his
very characters themselves of their freedom
and vitality.   Thus, to put it shortly, the
poet in him will make trees as lively as men,
while the next moment the philosopher in
him will make men as helpless as trees.

This is his strength and his weakness.
There is no escaping his philosophy in any
criticism of him because there is no escaping
it in reading him.   (For example, one of his
defects to a modern reader is his habit of
using scientific terms and analogies, indulging
in a kind of writing that makes a novel seem
startlingly new for ten years and then old-
fashioned in manner for ever afterwards.)
All his tragic tales show us human beings,
limited in every direction but their capacity

for suffering, caught in the great machine of
Nature or Law or Destiny.   But this machine
is a very curious one, for it does not toss out
ill fortune or good fortune blindly, as a
machine would ; it acts like a spirit, and
like a very malevolent spirit, who takes
pleasure in cruel ironies, sporting with its
Tesses as a cat plays with a mouse.   We are
not in a universe of immutable law but of
devilish whims : our destiny may be determined by a throw of the dice, but the dice
are always loaded against us.   Hardy seems
frequently contradictory just because he is so
bent on making the worst of things.   If
scientific determinism will do the trick, then
it may ;   but if it looks as if the prisoner were
going to escape, Hardy brings in a vindictive
" President of the Immortals " to see that
everything happens for the worst.   There
is something forced and false about his
tragedy that prevents us from accepting him
as one of the world's great tragedians.   When
we read of his Tess or Jude, we do not feel
that life itself is tragic in grain, and instead of

that exaltation that follows great tragedy, mere depression or irritation masters us and even drives out any feeling of pity. This is because Tess and Jude simply seem what lawyers call " hard cases." Moreover, the author's ironical manipulation of his figures, magnificent as it can be, frequently over-reaches itself : when his little creatures show signs of walking out of a trap, we see his great hand on the wires, jerking them back again. Not only is a good deal of the action far from seeming inevitable ; it involves a definite falsification of life. Thus—to take one example out of many—if, in a Hardy novel, A falls in love with B, this is the signal for B to fall in love with C, C with D, and D with A, a state of affairs that gives our ironist the opportunity he needs, but that takes us a long way from real life, in which people are not so obligingly perverse and interest calls out interest, love replies to love.

But when all is said, Hardy remains a great novelist. These massive chronicles of his, moving so slowly but so surely, large of bone and sinew, give us a whole pastoral world to roam about in: the dark, teeming earth itself is there, the spread of cloud and glimmer of stars; the very landscape is instinct with a huge brooding life; the peasants move to their tasks or gather together and talk with a humorous simplicity that has not been bettered since Shakespeare; farmers and soldiers and carriers go their ways and find themselves caught in comedy and tragedy; a host of women, shrews and coquettes and passionate dreamers and large, simple, and noble natures, all limned with humour and pity and truth; a world of homely tasks and familiar routine, of wages and work and rents and mortgages, and yet a world that is a stage of action, sometimes as complicated as the roots of a tree, sometimes as great and elemental as a thunderstorm. We could say much in praise of Hardy's construction, his command of atmosphere, his sense of drama, his creation of character, but if we admire the majesty and truth of the huge world he has created, we need say little more.

His mood may change—from the idyll of
Under the Greenwood Tree, the happy romanc-
ing of *Far from the Madding Crowd*, to the
stormy *Return of the Native* and the bitter
Tess of the D'Urbervilles—but that world, so
fully penetrated, so massively presented, is
the same. "It is the work of long thought
about familiar things : the two conditions of
the best writing," said Lionel Johnson, and
then added : " That deep solemnity of the
earth in its woods, and fields, and lonely
places, has passed into his work : and when
he takes it in hand, to deal with the passion
of men, that spirit directs and guides him."

Hardy's last and most ruthless novel, *Jude
the Obscure*, appeared in the middle of the
Nineties, and by this time fiction had taken
several new turns. The Victorian novel
(not excluding the work of Meredith and
Hardy) had been very English and even
insular; its size and fertility, its huge but
leisurely progress, its mingling of comic
and tragic elements, its digressions and
" asides " and " preaching," were all very

English. Perhaps the shortest way of describing the new kinds of fiction that appeared is to say that their authors intended them to be as unlike the Victorian novel as possible. It is usual to point out that during the Eighties and Nineties French influences, notably those of Flaubert, Maupassant, and Zola, were at work, leading to what is called Realism or Naturalism. But it is easier to make use of these terms than to define them, and, indeed, they are misleading. No writer can give all the facts, and these new realists selected just as rigorously, and in so doing indulged their own temperaments just as thoroughly as the Victorian masters had done. We may guess, however, what was in their minds when they called themselves Realists. They wished to give an appearance of strict verisimilitude to every incident and person in their narratives ; to avoid the silly names that the older novelists had given their minor characters, and the occasional preposterous incidents ; to keep themselves in the background and thus cut out all preaching, addresses to the reader, and so forth; to appear, in short, to be reporting and not to be inventing. In addition, they wished to give whatever facts seemed to them essential to the narrative, no matter how unpleasant those facts might be : they were, in truth, anxious to put forward the unpleasant facts. Again, they were determined not to follow the prudish restraint of the Victorians proper, but to deal more openly and candidly and sensibly with sexual matters. There began what has since been called the now-that-it-can-be-told school of fiction. The novel lost something of its old broad sweep and its zest, but it soon began to conquer new territory. It turned outward, exploiting vast stores of new material (such as the India that Rudyard Kipling brought to it); and it also turned inward, into the mind itself, whose fine shades of feeling, passing fancies, half-formed thoughts became the stuff out of which narratives could be made. This, then, is what was happening to the novel during the last twenty years of the

century, and all the novelists that follow
exhibit several of these changes in their
work, though not one of them shows them
all.

There is nothing Victorian about the way
in which Robert Louis Stevenson (1850–1894)
tells a story : his narratives, whether they
are purely romantic like *Treasure Island*,
historical romantic like *Catriona*, fantastic
like *The New Arabian Nights*, or gloriously
farcical like *The Wrong Box* (which is rarely
recognised for what it is, a little masterpiece
of high spirits), his narratives, whatever their
kind, have the poise and grace and concealed
strength of a fencer.   Stevenson is a very
curious figure.   For the last thirty years the
most ferocious attacks have been made upon
his reputation, and yet it keeps blithely on
its way.   The odd thing is that these adverse
criticisms of his fiction have been quite just,
pointing out many real and damaging weaknesses.   As a story-teller he is full of faults,
not the least of them the lack of that large
sincerity which always masters the reader's

imagination.   He never quite " found himself " in fiction, though there is evidence that
he might have done had he lived a little
longer.   Why is it, then, that his reputation
lives, that he is still read and enjoyed by the
wisest of men ?   The answer is, briefly, that
we are attracted to him as a personality.   He
had a most charming personality, and he had
the gift, rare enough to be called genius, of
making cold print the exquisite and tireless
servant of that personality.   His secret, in
life and literature, was his ability to make any
number of friends with either the spoken or
written word;   in short, charm.   And there
is nothing in more recent literature to suggest
that this supreme quality of his has become so
common that we can afford to ignore him.
The only people who can do that are those
who are insensitive to charm, and it is pity
that so many of them should be critics.
Among the admirers of Stevenson were
J. M. Barrie, who was the best of the sentimental Scottish or " Kailyard " school, and
" Q," who has every merit of a good story-

teller except constructive ability. Among
the writers who did not admire Stevenson
was an Irishman whose most impressionable
years were spent in Paris, George Moore
(1853–   ). George Moore's first period,
when, in *A Mummer's Wife* and *A Drama in
Muslin* and other things, he seems to be
trying to write a French novel in English,
and not always good English, reaches its
climax in 1894, when he published *Esther
Waters*, one of the best novels of the decade.
He had then an Irish period, during which
he was perfecting the curious prose style that
he has since put to such good uses in his third
and last period, the triumph of which has
undoubtedly been his story of Joseph of
Arimathea and Jesus and Paul, *The Brook
Kerith*. This style of his, with its long, slow
movement and cadences, its soft shimmer, is
perfectly fitted for reverie, and all his later
pieces of fiction have the quality and charm
of reveries. But these take us forward thirty
years. A contemporary of the earlier Moore
was George Gissing (1857–1903), whose

name, like Moore's, was at one time almost a war-cry among young men who believed in the " new realism." Gissing was a very sensitive and scholarly man whose circumstances denied him the life of culture and pleasant scholarship for which alone he was really fitted.   He was thrust into the dingiest and most depressing part of London, those shabby genteel and lower middle-class districts of North London that are far worse than the East End ; and with great sincerity and courage he wrote a series of novels (*Demos*, *The Nether World*, *New Grub Street*, *Born in Exile*, *The Odd Women*—such bitter titles tell their own tales), in which he gives his version of shabby genteel and lower middle-class life, and usually shows some sensitive soul fighting a losing battle with poverty and squalor and ugliness. His version, however, is obviously an attack and not an interpretation ; he is not sufficiently robust to deal fully and justly with the life he describes ; we feel that if he had peeped into the homes of the little clerks and workmen in Dickens (he had a great admiration for Dickens), he would have been so wincingly preoccupied with the sight of a dirty plate or a soiled towel that he would never have seen anything that Dickens saw. What he set down is true enough, but it is not—except for certain special people—the whole truth. He was himself a square peg in a round hole —for his whole nature cried out against his circumstances, and he took no pleasure in the raw material of his art—and his fiction is the sad chronicle of other square pegs. Incidentally this concern with the London scene is one of the marks of the time. Popular story-tellers like Walter Besant had already exploited the East End; and in the Nineties a number of novelists arrived to carve the city into slices, Zangwill taking the Jewish quarters, Pett Ridge and some others the unfashionable suburbs, and W. W. Jacobs, a humorist with a very narrow range, but a genuine and original artist, appropriating the docks.

There remains a novelist older than any of

those mentioned in the last paragraph, a novelist of great achievement and of still greater influence. This was Henry James (1843–1916). He was an American, but almost all his life was passed in Europe, chiefly in England, and he must be given a place here. It is impossible to present any adequate idea of his peculiar genius in a few sentences. His literary life was a long one, and he was for ever making experiments, so that the Henry James of *Roderick Hudson* (1875) is not the Henry James of *The Wings of the Dove* (1902) and *The Ambassadors* (1903). There is, however, a steady development in his work. We have said that the Novel turned inward, discovering that fine shades of feeling, the more subtle antics of the mind, were themselves an adventure. Meredith helped to give the Novel this turn, and was successful sometimes in presenting a scene completely from the point of view of one of the actors in it. Henry James went much further in this direction than Meredith. He made comedy and tragedy out of shades and flickers of thought and feeling. His people themselves and the whole life he describes are sophisticated, self-conscious, introspective, subtle, and the narratives that present these people and comment on this life are compelled to exhibit a still more sophisticated and subtle intelligence. He has to make art out of people who have already turned life itself into an art. Thus he seems the most studiously artificial of all novelists, one who admits us into a world of smiling or tortured ghosts. He was himself a man without roots, one of those cultured Americans who carefully exile themselves and wander from Paris to London, London to Rome, untroubled by business or politics or any passion except curiosity, which becomes a passion in the absence of any large competing interests. Even their deep concern for art is a part of this curiosity ; they want to *know* about the beautiful. Henry James has been praised for his knowledge of classes and races, moral traditions, and social codes ; the truth is, however, that though his peculiar position enabled him to explore many different kinds of European society, he never really understood any of them because he did not know the roots that fed them. He was only really at home (and we never think of his being " at home," for he is essentially homeless) with the cultured cosmopolitan society, the hothouse blooms of the garden. His birth and traditions were American or, rather, Bostonian ; his literary affinities were French ; and most of his life was spent in England, a country he loved but did not really understand. Thus he lived rootless, in mid-air, in decided contrast with such a novelist as Hardy, whose power seems to come from the very earth itself of his home. But this curious situation enabled James to concentrate more intensely on certain matters, those interests that remained. One of them, as we have seen, was the delicate tragi-comedy of the mind of man in a highly complex social life. Another was the art of fiction itself, which was a passion with him, and he brought to the consideration of its problems—how a narrative might be told, a scene presented—all the power of his strong and subtle mind. He made more deliberate and successful experiments than any novelist who ever lived, and he is able at times to make both novel-writing and novel-reading seem an exciting adventure, simply on account of the craft itself. At other times, however, he seems over-literary; we smell nothing but ink and paper in some stories of his, novels about novelists for novelists, a kind of literary cannibalism. Not least, he has a style, very elaborate and with clause within clause like an Oriental nest of boxes, that is not easy to read and can be very exasperating, but a style that is amazingly successful because it can express the finest of fine shades and also creates almost at once his own peculiar atmosphere; it leads us, curious and delicately tiptoeing, straight into the Henry James world. And that world, for all its artificiality and finicking, reveals more surely and subtly than that of any other novelist certain minor phases of human comedy and tragedy : we begin by seeming to turn our backs on reality, but we come at times to the very heart of it.

CHAPTER VII

THE FICTION OF TO-DAY

TIME is the best literary critic. It would be impossible to write a brief account of such a colossal subject as this if Time had not done most of the work first. But now that we have arrived at the present century, Time is no longer able to help us, being still too busy piling up names and volumes. A whole big book, written so near to the roaring scene of action, could not adequately survey the novels of the last twenty-five years, and to do it in one tiny chapter is a hopeless task. If we are asked, " What has been happening to the English Novel during this period ? " we are tempted to reply, " Everything ! " and to let it go at that. The English Novel has continued to do all the things that we saw it begin doing in the last two chapters.   It has laid hands on more and more of life, though this does not mean that individual novels have had a greater range and sweep than those of past generations. All that it means is that when, for example, sociology was in the air, we had sociological fiction, when psycho-analysis arrived, we very soon were given psycho-analytical novels. A great many contemporary novelists are more like journalists than story-tellers, for their chief desire is to reflect the interests of the moment and their concern with character and action is very slight. Then, again, the older kinds of fiction still persist ; the novel of Jane Austen, the Early Victorian, and the Mid-Victorian novels, are still being written ; we recognise the sources of the novelists' inspiration, the origins of their methods, though their work is naturally different because their material is different. Such a novelist as Archibald Marshall is obviously handling twentieth-century life in a certain traditional manner, and the result is quite amusing.   Recently, some young writers have returned to an eighteenth-century manner. William de Morgan, who did not begin writing fiction until he was an old man, returned quite naturally in *Joseph Vance* and *Alice-for-Short* to the fog and fun and rambling length of the Mid-Victorian novel. Maurice Hewlett took the familiar historical romance and in *Richard-Yea-and-Nay* and *The Queen's Quair* (his masterpiece) gave it a new subtlety. In addition, quite a number of writers of originality and unusual power have turned to fiction and given us stories that are not very successful strictly considered as novels but yet are valuable, sometimes unique performances, more dear to us perhaps than other more imposing works of fiction because they express personalities that delight us. Among these writers are W. H. Hudson, Kenneth Grahame, Walter de la Mare, G. K. Chesterton, James Stephens. Samuel Butler is possibly one of them. His satirical and largely autobiographical *Way of All Flesh* has been put forward as one of the greatest

5

novels of the age, chiefly because its powerful
attack upon what some people imagine to be
typically Victorian religious thought, educa-
tion, and family life, exactly hit the taste of
the time.   And this is a fact worth remem-
bering, for a good deal of contemporary
criticism of fiction completely overlooks the
novelist as artist in favour of the novelist as
social critic and theorist.

If we compare the mass of intelligent
fiction of the last twenty years with the bulk
of nineteenth-century fiction, we notice a
marked difference in the attitudes of the two
sets of novelists.   Briefly, it is this.   The
older novelists wanted to tell a story, to
describe an action, to let us know what
happened to Tom and Mabel; they began
a definite narrative in the first chapter and
rounded it off in the last; they were anxious
to be as life-like as possible, but they were
determined to impose some particular pattern
of event upon life, shaping it decisively to
suit the purposes of their particular art.   But
many of the novelists of to-day do not

approach fiction in this way at all. For the story, the ordered action, they substituted what has been called the " slice of life." They do not try to tell us what happened to Tom and Mabel, but how life appeared to Tom or Mabel for a season. " I suppose what I am trying to render is nothing more nor less than Life—as one man has found it. I want to tell—*myself*, and my impressions of the thing as a whole, to say things I have come to feel intensely of the laws, traditions, usages, and ideas we call society, and how we poor individuals get driven and lured and stranded among these windy, perplexing shoals and channels." This is from H. G. Wells, and it is a fair statement of his aims. He has wandered so far from the traditional outlook of the novelist that he can remark, in another place : " I do not see why I should always pander to the vulgar appetite for stark stories." (And a very silly remark it is, too. The appetite for stark stories is just as vulgar as the appetite for plain food, and compares very favourably with the appetite for easy and hasty generalisations about everything.) It is this attempt first and foremost to " render Life " that is the mark of contemporary fiction. The older novelists, like Wells, are concerned with those " laws, traditions, usages, and ideas we call society "; and the slices of life they give us have been frequently cut from the week-old loaf of sociology. But the younger novelists have concentrated upon the " I want to tell— *myself* "; and they have almost literally given the reader a piece of their minds. They have tried to capture the wild bird of life in a net made up of every impression, passing fancy, flicker of thought in the mind. With the older slicers of life, character and action were not treated too well, but with the younger ones, they practically disappear, leaving us a curious kind of fiction in which nobody does anything very much, and one person is no different from another. We have to be content with following the stream of consciousness, the endless rush of thoughts and images in one person's mind. The manner has its own triumphant moments, but it demands too great a sacrifice of character and drama, and it very soon becomes monotonous. But it is probably the logical conclusion of the " slice of life " method, which was ready to jettison so much that was once thought necessary in fiction in order to present the very texture of our ordinary life. At first it was our life from day to day, but now it is from moment to moment: the novelists who have adopted this method can now go no further without ceasing to be intelligible : they are in a blind alley. The slice of life has now come to be very indigestible. So much for the drift of English fiction during these last twenty years.

We will begin with Joseph Conrad, who was the senior of all the novelists still to be mentioned. He is perhaps the strangest figure in the history of the English novel. A Polish aristocrat, born out of sight and sound of the sea, he became a master-mariner in the English merchant service. This in itself was a tremendous feat. Then this foreigner, writing laboriously in our difficult language, this retired sea-captain, turned novelist, and became one of the greatest personalities in modern fiction. He forged for himself a style that was never perhaps quite happy in individual strokes, but that was almost unmatched in its power of conjuring up romantic atmospheres of every kind. For years he had, as it were, soaked in such atmospheres. And for years, too, he had brooded over the characters and destinies of men. The little lighted deck of a ship is close and familiar, but beyond the rail, only a hand's breadth away, there is the mystery of the sea; and Conrad saw life in these terms. With all the outward interest and excitement of the romantic narrative, he combined the inward excitement of the psychological story; he took his readers to the Indian Ocean and the Islands, showed them strangely coloured skies and seas, mysterious brown and yellow faces, but at the same time he took them by devious ways into the minds of men, went in search of the soul as if he were stalking a ghost. What interests him is the mind of a man, an Almayer, a Captain McWhirr, an Axel Heyst, in relation to a certain event, the two, man and event, conceived in a certain atmosphere, and the whole thing bodying forth his heroic-tragic vision of life. His figures are very sharply drawn, are distinct individuals, but there always comes a time when they shed their individuality and become symbolical, typifying the whole race of men. "Those who read me," he once wrote, "know my conviction that the world, the temporal world, rests on a few very simple ideas : so simple that they must be as old as the hills. It rests notably, among others, on the idea of Fidelity." The soul of man heroically defying a mysteriously hostile universe is his theme : a ship against the background of the night. "We live as we dream—alone," he has said ; and most of his stories show us men, isolated and bewildered, frequently going down before the meaningless blows delivered out of the darkness, but keeping

some word passed by the soul. His is
essentially a man's world : his women are
only shadowy, smiling figures, waiting for
news ; there is no successful full-length
portrait of a woman in any story of his, not
even in *The Arrow of Gold*, in which he very
obviously made the attempt to paint such a
portrait. But his men are magnificent. He
also made great play with a curiously indirect
method of telling a story, a method that is
sometimes rather tiresome but that enabled
him to present us with scenes of astonishing
vividness and force against a fragmentary
kind of background that creates the illusion
of life. Some of the more tragic tales gain
in poignancy by being related in an apparent
jumble (though really, of course, a most
artful selection) of bits of gossip, odd
impressions, picked up on the verandas of
Eastern hotels and officers' clubs. Our
news of these tragic personages seems to
filter through slowly as news must do in real
life ; we have to scan the whole world for
them, picking up their trails here and there.

In this, and other matters, Conrad's influence has been immense, and he is easily the greatest romantic artist in modern fiction.

What exactly H. G. Wells is nobody can say. There can be no doubt whatever that he is a man of literary genius, whose mind is sometimes a dynamo of genuine creative energy. Wells has spent a great deal of his time acting as an intellectual irritant, in which capacity he has aroused the dislike of people who do not want to think and has also exasperated the people who have long been in the habit of thinking. On the other hand, there are masses of people whom he has taught to question life, and not to accept things on trust, and as popular educator, journalist, and social prophet, Wells is undoubtedly one of the great figures of the contemporary world. As a novelist proper, he is a much smaller figure, perhaps one that is still shrinking, but nevertheless his reputation is safe enough. There are, first, the scientific romances and short stories, which are incomparably the best things of their kind

5*

ever written.   One or two of them, notably *The Invisible Man* among the long tales, and *The Country of the Blind* among the short tales, are masterpieces.   Then there are the two stories in which his knowledge of lower middle-class life and his creative exuberance are at work together : *Kipps* and *The History of Mr. Polly*.   Both these wistful and comic draper's assistants are at once real and delightful characters, whose adventures we follow with zest, and typical figures of our age, which Wells as usual (and for once successfully) attacks for its muddle and waste. Then there are his wide panoramas of the social scene, of which the best is easily *Tono Bungay*, that epic history of a patent medicine which contrives to pass in review the whole England of its day.   Wells has the temperament of a romantic idealist plus the training and interests of a scientist, and to that combination we owe his peculiar genius in fiction, but to that also we owe his almost permanent mood of exasperation that has left him contemptuous and impatient of art, including the art he has practised. He has always been so angry with the world for its waste and muddle that he has forgotten that his first duty is not to waste his own great gifts and muddle the one thing he happens to be doing in the world. Had he been as whole-hearted and conscientious about his own chosen work, that of writing novels, as the engineers and scientists he praises are about theirs, his achievement would have been immeasurably greater. As it is, it is very substantial, never flawless but frequently touched with real genius.

Arnold Bennett has not the creative energy, the immense fertility of Wells, but he has the gift, which Wells has not, of making the most of his gifts. He is, in short, the better artist. This is partly because he very early came under French influences, and began writing fiction as an admirer of those naturalistic novelists who made much of " technique "— that is, a detached point of view, a suppression of the narrator, a deliberate simplicity and unity in the action and background. His mind, with its robust common sense, its complete lack of any mystical or even strongly idealistic elements, its generalising habit, has certain affinities with the typical French mind. It is possible, too, that it was contact with French life and art that sharpened his sense of the dramatic and gave to his handling of a scene a certain lightness and crispness.   But if his literary " nurture " has been French, his " nature " is English : his roots are in the provincial and industrial England of the Midlands and the North.   He has all the typical qualities of the urban provincial in excess : he is alert, humorous, curious and knowing, aggressively self-confident, and ambitious, but never losing a fine boyish wonder.   His lighter novels, such as *The Card* and *The Regent*, show him exploiting these qualities and the provincial humours of his own district, the Five Towns.   The Five Towns is one of the grimmest and ugliest of all industrial districts, and it is Bennett's delight (and ours, too, to follow him) to run a kind of romantic obstacle race, carefully to put aside all the usual picturesque trappings and then to evolve, against odds, romance itself. This he does to our admiration, though there are times when he forces the note, when he has, so to speak, to put in too many exclamation marks. His more sustained and serious novels carry on this work on a higher level. The best of them, *The Old Wives' Tale*, a really massive work of art, describes the lives of two sisters, who slowly change before our eyes from being lively young girls to helpless old women. If we think first of the young girls, then the tale is a grim tragedy; but if we think first (as the author did) of the dull old women and then realise that they have marched through this epic, then the tale is a romance. As one or the other, its firm lines, its huge social background, its spirit of grave pity, make it one of the capital achievements of modern fiction. There is nothing else so good in Bennett, though *Clayhanger* (the first volume of an ambitious trilogy that unfortunately did not succeed) and *Riceyman Steps*, a grim study of a miser, have something of the same rare quality. All these things are like paintings of the Flemish School, full of solidly real things and a sober daylight that has in it just a glint of romance. The rest of his tales are like spirited sketches of life in the Five Towns and London, apt to be repetitious and too generalising (thus all his men and women are in love with one another in exactly the same way until the relation becomes a formula with him), but crammed with excellent observation and humour and a sort of poetry of streets, hotels, emporiums. Arnold Bennett is at once the historian, the philosopher, and the troubadour of our ordinary urban life.

It is a mistake to imagine that John Galsworthy, whose best work is to be found in that series of novels now called *The Forsyte Saga*, is simply a Bennett with an upper-middle-class and country gentleman background. Bennett, who is either serenely detached or humorously sympathetic, interprets his chosen people, but Galsworthy, hurt and angry, attacks or defends. It is his weakness as an artist that he does not put his characters on a stage but puts some on the bench and the rest in the dock. He takes sides. He is so angry with the unimaginative, cautious but greedy Forsytes, so passionate an ally of the rebels, the bohemians, the lovers of beauty, that he loses something of his own exquisite sensitiveness and becomes at times the crudest of satirists and ironists. But when the creative artist in him gains the upper hand and he can take delight in the mere recording, then his picture of the Forsyte family, with every detail of whose life he has the fullest acquaintance, becomes one of the notable things of modern fiction. Old Jolyon Forsyte and Soames Forsyte (particularly in the later stories) are fully articulated human beings, creatures all too rare in fiction. But what perhaps distinguishes Galsworthy is his ability to present convincingly what might be called the "mechanics" of our social life (for *The Forsyte Saga* is an epic of property-owning), crowding the scene with real shareholders' meetings and solicitors' offices, and at the same time to suggest a background of passionate desire and wistful dream, beauty troubling this grimly possessive world. Galsworthy has an epic breadth, is a very sound designer, and, though sensitive, is never subtle; and if we wish to find a complete contrast we shall find it in the work of E. M. Forster, who cares little or nothing for breadth and sound design and is impishly subtle. He is the first of the later novelists, perhaps the first of the strictly modern school, his approach to his art being quite different from that of Wells or Bennett or Galsworthy. He is not anxious to paint a convincing picture of the world, setting out in order all the surface realities; and all his novels (the best are *A Room with a View*, *Howards End*, and *A Passage to India*) contain absurd and incredible incidents, and some characters that are nothing but vague outlines; and there is something freakish, invalidish, intellectually finicking, about his world, in which will and passion hardly exist. Compared with his seniors, those sober and

massive chroniclers, he is like an elf making
odd comments on this world, for ever con-
trasting the outer life and the inner life.   His
very style seems disjointed, careless.   It is,
however, exquisitely turned for its purpose,
which is not that of description but evocation ;
he uses it to bring before us the essentials of
the matter, the heart of a mood, the whole
atmosphere of a time, a place ; he is always
aiming at some inner and essential reality, and
when he gives us the illusion of having
reached it with him, as he does quite frequently, he completely captures our imagination.   Incidentally, this method of his, which
consists in keeping aloof most of the time and
then suddenly diving right into the depths of
a character's mind, is artistically sounder,
certainly less wearisome, than the later
" stream of consciousness " method already
described.   This latter is the method we find
in *Portrait of the Artist as a Young Man* and (at
its maddest) in *Ulysses*, both by James Joyce,
who has real power and originality, but a
mind at once warped and pedantic, like that

of a barbarian who has been suddenly given an overdose of civilisation. A more delicate use of the method can be seen in Virginia Woolf's novels, especially *Mrs. Dalloway* and *To the Lighthouse*, which are like rapid coloured films that have occasional moments of great poignancy.

But all these writers of our own time can wait for other and larger volumes to do them justice. There is space here for little more than a bare mention of their names. Among the women novelists there is that cool feminine wit renowned as the author of *Elizabeth and Her German Garden*; there is May Sinclair, very sincere, packed with thought, a trifle arid, and with the shadow of the psychologist or psycho-analyst falling too often across her page; there is Ethel Sidgwick, whose comedies suggest a curious mixture of Jane Austen and Meredith; and Sheila Kaye-Smith, who has fully penetrated the life of the Sussex countryside, and whose earlier work especially is good, solid story-telling; and the late Katherine Mansfield, whose short stories show a real if limited genius. Somerset Maugham must be given a high place among the remaining male novelists, not so much as the author of some admirably deft short stories and short novels, but as the author of that full yet austere chronicle, one of the best auto-biographical novels of this age, *Of Human Bondage*. Then there is that group of novelists who were all "young men of promise" just before the war, and have since been busy confounding or confirming the prophets. Neither J. D. Beresford nor Oliver Onions belongs to this group, how-ever; both are of robust masculine temper and have done good work in various directions, but have never yet succeeded in producing the respective masterpieces that would fully exhibit all their excellent quali-ties. Its most disappointing member is pro-bably Compton Mackenzie, who began well with such things as *Carnival* and *Sinister Street*, written in a style full of perfume and glitter (sometimes that of cheap scent and spangles) and presenting one side of London life better than it had ever been presented before; but has never been able to grow up into a serious artist. Gilbert Cannan, too, never fulfilled the fiery promise of his youth. This cannot be said of D. H. Lawrence, now one of the gods of the young intellectuals and a writer very much over-praised in some quarters. His range is extraordinarily narrow, and he has begun to repeat himself and even to parody himself; his sense of character is not very strong, and he is often content to give us very little action and a good deal of aimless talk; but, on the other hand, his tense and vivid prose can completely capture any and every kind of physical sensation and also suggest all the dark promptings of what we call the unconscious, whose mysterious activities, chiefly with regard to sex, are usually his theme. Very foolishly he has tried to philosophise upon instead of merely describing these orgiastic impulses: he is the poet of a world in rut, and lately he has become its prophet with unfortunate results

in his fiction. Then there is Francis Brett
Young, an excellent romancer in such things
as *The Tragic Bride* and *The Black Diamond*,
who has recently shown by his *Portrait of
Clare*, a fine, large picture of English country
life, that he may yet become one of our
major novelists; and there is Frank Swinner-
ton, whose novels of suburban London are
in the Arnold Bennett tradition, but whose
little masterpiece *Nocturne* is all his own, a
capital achievement. And, not least, there
is Hugh Walpole, who, despite some mani-
fest inequalities in his work, moves steadily
forward. His worst fault is a looseness of
grip upon his art (showing itself in bad
construction and too easy writing), the result
probably of being so generously endowed
with the various gifts of a story-teller that
each narrative gallops away with him. But
though he can certainly be accused of having
taken things far too easily, you can find in his
best work, from the nerve-storm of *Mr.
Perrin and Mr. Traill* to the delicate comedy
of *The Green Mirror*, the large crowded canvas

of *The Cathedral* to the grey miniature of *The Old Ladies*, an unusually wide range of those qualities that may not make the philosopher, the poet, or the prophet, but that certainly make the good novelist. There is in his work, which shows signs of further development, an attempt to grapple with the whole social scene and a determination to lose sight neither of character nor story that connect him with the main tradition of the English Novel.

We have done now with names, but there is space for a word or two concerning the newest fiction, the work of the latest generation of novelists. So far it chiefly expresses the prevailing mood of disillusion and exasperation, sometimes in deep seriousness, but often, and more effectively, in a spirit of rather bitter comedy. These younger writers are still too busy explaining themselves and giving life a piece of their minds to explain other people and give their minds a piece of life. In short, they are commentators rather than creative dramatic artists. We find in their work innumerable clever remarks and some admirable passages of autobiography, but very few characters of any importance and little attempt to construct a significant action. It is, indeed, the day of clever little novels, the cocktails and sandwiches of fiction. The large-scale realism of the older novelists has been replaced either by completely subjective or " stream of consciousness " novels or (possibly in reaction against these) by rather brittle and fantastic narratives that are more or less symbolical. Much of the fiction of the last two generations was the work of social critics and rebels, who challenged the existing order and various religious and political beliefs; but the newest generation, arriving at maturity in that atmosphere of dis-illusion and weariness which so often follows a great war, can neither destroy nor build, accept nor reject, and so have turned aside from that consideration of man in society which bears such excellent fruit in the novel. Unfortunately, being introspective com-mentators rather than dramatic artists, they find it difficult to body forth anything but the antics of their own minds, which, however, the best of them do with commendable and devastating honesty. All this may be right and necessary, but it is a misfortune for the Novel, which asks for something more than elaborate introspection or the charity that begins and stays at home. If you are determined not to be taken in by life, as these younger writers so obviously are, you may be many things, but it is not likely that you will be a novelist of any importance. The major novelist succeeds because, for the purpose of his art at least, he is taken in at every turn by life, by the hopes and fears, the joy and sorrow, of all manner of fellow-creatures. It is this wide sympathy, this brave generosity of the imagination, that lies at the root of all great fiction, and at the moment it is not much in evidence. But that does not necessarily mean that the English Novel, which has had such a long and glorious history, is about to say good-bye to great names and great achievements, that the fire of it will soon be nothing but a shower of little sparks.   If there is one thing that history teaches us, it is the folly of indulging in premature head-shaking.   Many a good critic of the past has come to cut a foolish figure in our eyes because he gravely announced that something was all over when, in truth, we know now that it was only just beginning.   A hundred years ago, when Jane Austen had been dead ten years and Scott had done his best work and scribblers like Hook represented the art of fiction, it might well have been thought, as indeed it was thought, that the English Novel was declining into mediocrity.   The critics little imagined that it was about to enter into what is perhaps its greatest period; and our prophetic powers are no greater than theirs.   The English Novel may yet pour out treasure in the old generous fashion; and if it does not, we shall not be poor, for it has already left us a gigantic and imperishable legacy.

BIBLIOGRAPHICAL NOTE

THE Novel has its place, though not always a sufficiently important place, in all histories of English literature, and there is no need to enumerate these. There are surprisingly few volumes of any importance entirely devoted to the Novel. Sir Walter Raleigh's *English Novel* (John Murray) only takes us as far as Jane Austen and Scott, but is worth reading for its excellent studies of the eighteenth-century novelists. Mr. George Saintsbury's book on the Novel in Dent's *Channels of English Literature* series covers nearly everything up to about 1890, and is especially valuable on the historical side. Mr. Gerald Bullett's *Modern English Fiction* (Herbert Jenkins) is a very compact and well-written study of the contemporary novel, and there are some lively discussions on the subject in Miss Elizabeth Drew's *The Modern*

Novel (Cape).   By far the best book on the peculiar art of the novelist, the technique of narration, is Mr. Percy Lubbock's *Craft of Fiction* (Cape), though the ordinary reader might perhaps be advised to begin with Mr. Arnold Bennett's *The Author's Craft* (Hodder and Stoughton) and Mrs. Wharton's *The Writing of Fiction* (Scribners).   It is hardly necessary to say that, in such series as the *English Men of Letters*, and elsewhere, there may be found separate volumes, biographical or critical, on nearly all the more important English novelists.

J. B. P.